HALF TRUTH

A SQUEAKY CLEAN IN BETWEEN MYSTERY
BOOK 2.5

CHRISTY BARRITT

NOTE TO READERS:

If you're an avid Squeaky Clean series reader, this book officially takes place between *It Came Upon a Midnight Crime* and *Organized Grime*.

CHAPTER ONE

I RAISED my hand in the air as I felt opportunity begin to slip away. "One hundred dollars!"

My breath clouded with frost in front of me as I stood outside on the cold thirty-seven-degree day. At least it was sunny. And at least I was surrounded by a wall of lime green storage units to break the wind.

An auctioneer stood at the front of the crowd.

I'd envisioned going to an auction before. But in my imaginings, people had been dressed in tuxes and fancy dresses while bidding on famous paintings and artwork.

This was more of a redneck auction, with most of the crowd seeming rather ordinary in their jeans and sweatshirts.

I fit in here.

These were my people.

Ordinary people. Blue-collar people.

I'd convinced myself that the contents of Unit 139 should be mine.

Don't ask me why. I'd just decided I wanted what was behind that roll-up door.

Riley Thomas, my friend, neighbor, and the man I was secretly crushing on, leaned closer. "You could pay your electric bill for the month with that money, you know."

"I realize that. But I just *know* something good is inside that storage unit. Besides, it's the last one I can bid on." For no good reason, I'd chickened out before bidding on the previous ten units that had been up for auction.

Money wasn't something I played around with—especially since I lived from paycheck to paycheck.

But I considered this a business opportunity. I was hoping this place would be packed with items that I could resell on eBay or even at a yard sale. Maybe someone had even left money inside.

I'd heard of crazier things happening.

Somehow, I'd talked Riley into coming with me to this auction where the contents of unpaid storage units were being sold. Usually, the auctioneer gave people a peek inside the units before bidding began.

This time, he was selling them all sight unseen—

almost as mystery offers, I supposed. And I *loved* mysteries.

I couldn't wait to see what was inside Unit 139 of the Excess Storage Facility in Norfolk, Virginia.

I'd heard about these auctions for a long time, and it had been on my bucket list to actually come to one of these events and bid on a unit. I wasn't even quite sure why—other than the suspense of it all.

Also, I wanted to do something different, something exciting. This seemed like a better option than, let's say . . . hang gliding or going to a casino.

"One twenty-five," a man behind me said.

Surprise washed through me when I heard the competing bid.

I turned to look at the guy who'd called out the amount and saw he was wearing a black baseball cap, sunglasses, and a puffy black jacket that concealed most of his features.

He'd been at the auction from the start. I'd seen him in the crowd when I signed in.

But he hadn't bid on any of the other storage units. Only this one.

Since each unit was being sold sight unseen, why was that? Why was he only bidding on this one? Did he know something I didn't?

Then again . . . he could be thinking the same thing about me. I shouldn't rush to judgment.

Determination rose in me. "One fifty!"

"One seventy-five," the man called back.

We'd been instructed to bid in twenty-five-dollar increments.

"Two hundred!" I wasn't sure what was happening to me. Did I really want this storage unit that bad? Or did I just want to win?

Either way, I was all in. Some type of determination had grown inside me, almost like a sports car going from zero to sixty in 5.2 seconds.

I glanced over my shoulder at the man, waiting to see if he would outbid me again.

I couldn't see his eyes. Couldn't see if he was looking at me or tell what he was thinking.

A fact that kind of drove me crazy. I liked trying to read people, and I'd become pretty good at it. Sunglasses made that hard.

"Three hundred," the man said.

I sucked in a breath. He'd skipped two twenty-five, two fifty, and two seventy-five!

"Gabby . . ." Riley muttered as if he were reading my mind and knew exactly what I was about to do.

"Four hundred!" I blurted.

Four hundred? Had I lost my mind? No one else had bid this high on other storage units. They'd maxed out at three hundred.

I needed my money to live on. I needed to eat, for goodness' sake!

But I would recoup the funds. I was sure of it.

I held my breath as I waited. Would the man bid against me again?

I heard nothing.

My gaze went back to the auctioneer, a bearded man who reminded me of a silver-tongued Grizzly Adams.

I wanted to win.

And I didn't want to win.

Part of me wanted to keep my hard-earned money.

The other part of me didn't want to lose.

I was such a mess at times.

"Four hundred dollars. Going once, going twice. Sold to the woman in the red coat and flip-flops."

At least that's what I *thought* he said. People said *I* talked fast, but this guy was giving me a run for my money.

I raised my hands in the air and let out a triumphant whoop. Then I turned to Riley and threw my arms around him as if I'd just won the million-dollar lottery. Instead, I'd purchased a storage unit sight unseen.

Despite that, I exclaimed, "I got it!"

He gave me a look before uncertainly asking, "Congratulations?"

"The sky is the limit right now. This is like a John Michael Montgomery song."

"Huh?" His blue eyes lit with confusion. He looked adorable as he tilted his head, his brown hair blowing in the light breeze.

"You know . . . 'The Grundy County Auction Incident' song?"

He twisted his head. "Never heard it."

"You'd totally recognize it if I sang it." So I did.

Riley's expression remained blank. As people stared at us, he might even be a little embarrassed.

I waved him off. "Anyway . . . I think that song was the inspiration for me being here today."

I resisted the urge to look back at the man I'd just beat. That would seem like gloating.

Instead, I just barely glanced over my shoulder.

The guy was gone.

Weird.

Maybe he was mad and had stormed off. I'd won fair and square, and now there was nothing he could do.

Before I could see what treasures I'd won, I had to go through several more procedures, including paying in cash.

That was when I realized I only had three hundred dollars with me.

I frowned. I'd been caught up in the moment, and I hadn't even thought through how I was going to pay for this.

Just as I was contemplating what to do, Riley slapped some cash on the counter. "You can pay me back later."

"Really?" I searched his face, trying to figure out if he was serious.

"Really."

"Thank you," I rushed.

That could have been really embarrassing.

The storage facility employee reminded me that I only had twenty-four hours to either clean out the space or rent it myself. I had to turn in any personal items so they could be returned to the previous tenant, yada yada yada.

So many rules.

No desire to listen.

I just wanted to get inside my unit and see what I'd purchased.

Finally, the woman handed me the key. A zing zipped through me as I held it in my hands.

This was it. The moment I found out what was inside.

The crowd around me had dispersed, either

heading to whatever unit they won or heading to the parking lot to contend with their losses.

I turned and heard several people oohing and awing as they opened their units. I saw rooms filled from top to bottom with boxes and furniture. I heard people mention antiques. Baseball cards. Someone even had a motorcycle inside theirs.

A motorcycle!

Dollar signs flashed in my eyes.

I gripped the key as I turned to Riley. "Are you ready for this?"

"I can't wait."

I couldn't tell if he was being sarcastic or not, but I'd assume he was being sincere.

"Let's go." I headed toward my unit.

———

I paused in front of 139 and sucked in a deep breath of anticipation.

This was it.

The moment I'd been dreaming about.

The moment I'd open my figurative treasure chest and find out exactly what was inside.

I stared at the lime green garage door a brief second, feeling as if I'd won the pot of gold at the end of the rainbow.

I hoped I wasn't getting ahead of myself.

I needed to see exactly what my four hundred dollars had just purchased me.

I thrust my key into the lock and twisted.

Sucking in one more deep breath, I glanced at Riley. "Here goes nothing."

I used my palms to push the door up.

The inside of the storage unit came into view.

The *nearly empty* storage unit.

Nearly empty except for a banker's box sitting in the center of the floor.

One box? That was all that was inside?

One measly little box?

The air left my lungs.

My dreams of making a fortune on eBay dissipated faster than last week's paycheck.

"Maybe there's something valuable inside the box." Riley crept closer, his voice light as if he didn't want to upset me more than I already was.

But his words sounded weak.

He hadn't thought this auction was a good idea.

Maybe he was right.

One box?

I shook my head.

I couldn't get over it. I'd fully expected this unit to be loaded from top to bottom with someone's possessions. That was how most storage units looked. At least it was according to the shows I'd seen on TV.

"Are you going to open it?" Riley studied me as if trying to gauge my emotional state.

"You know it." I tried to sound more enthusiastic than I actually felt.

My feet dragged a little as I walked toward the box.

There wouldn't be hours and hours of digging through things as I'd envisioned. I had imagined most of my weekends being taken up at this place. That I'd find some valuables for resale. Or that I'd at least be able to have a yard sale to recoup my expenses.

At no time had I considered that I'd literally be throwing money down the drain.

I needed to make this more of a moment. For that reason, I sat down beside the box. I was going to take my time as I opened the top and pulled out whatever was inside very slowly.

If I wasn't going to make my money back, at least I could entertain myself for a few minutes.

Four hundred dollars for a few minutes of entertainment. I was ashamed of myself for my rash decision to bid above my pay grade. I could have used that money for so many other things.

No risk, no reward? Wasn't that what people

said?

Clearly, that advice wasn't always true.

This had been a terrible idea.

Riley squatted across from me on the other side of the box and waited.

I stared at the box another moment. The cardboard sides were ratty and beat-up—not exactly like a box that would hold anything valuable.

"Knowing my luck, there will be old dirty underwear and expired canned food inside," I muttered.

"Underwear and canned food?" Riley stared at me as if wondering why in the world I had picked those two things.

I shrugged because I wasn't really sure. "I've seen some really weird things in my line of work."

He knew that fact good and well. We'd been friends long enough that he was aware of my shenanigans as a crime scene cleaner. I saw the worst parts of a person's life. The parts that were left in the aftermath, many times in the aftermath of crime.

I sucked in a breath and looked at the box in front of me again.

I'd put this off for too long.

I still had hope that there would be something amazing inside and that this auction wouldn't be a total disappointment.

I knew from the moment I touched the box that

it wasn't loaded with anything. The box shifted in a way that made it clear. It wasn't full. Not even close.

Despite that, I pulled the top of the box off.

I stared at the contents and frowned.

On top was a partially opened map, which concealed whatever was below it.

The folded paper didn't look particularly old like a treasure map, but it didn't really look new and mass-produced either.

I knew these units went up for auction after sixty days of being unpaid. So someone could have left this here recently.

I carefully removed the map and placed it on the floor beside me. The next thing I saw was a professional-looking camera. The device was more than a point and shoot, at least—but I didn't know much about cameras.

"I might get some money off of this." My words sounded weak to my own ears.

"You might," Riley agreed.

I hit the power button, but nothing happened. The battery must be dead.

I set the camera aside also.

Something that appeared to be an old T-shirt lay at the bottom. But as I lifted it, I realized something had been wrapped inside the clothing.

My eyes widened when I realized it was . . . a small metal box.

Was this the treasure I'd been dreaming about finding?

"Maybe this is it," I murmured.

Maybe it was a collection of fine jewelry.

Diamonds would fit in a box this size.

Or gold. Gold would work. I wasn't picky.

I lifted it out, moved the banker's box out of the way, and set the metal box in front of me.

Then I gingerly pressed the latch to open it.

Nothing happened.

I tried again.

Still nothing.

"Gabby?" Riley murmured.

"It's locked."

"Can I try?" He reached for it.

"Of course." But if that box opened for him instead of me . . .

He pressed the release latch also, but the top stayed in place.

"It's definitely locked," he said as he studied it. "We can probably pick it."

"Or beat it with a hammer."

"How about we try to pick it first?"

"Probably a good idea," I conceded before letting out a sigh. "Well, this was a bust."

"I'm sorry."

Then my gaze caught the shirt that had been wrapped around the box. The clothing was beige with a small logo reading "FCB" off-center on the front.

Was that . . . ?

I lifted it and held it up.

Little specks of reddish brown were splattered on the front.

"Are you thinking what I'm thinking?" Riley stared at the shirt with a frown.

I couldn't tear my gaze away either. "Only if you're thinking that might be . . . blood."

CHAPTER
TWO

I STARED AT THE SHIRT, unsure what to say.

"It's not necessarily blood." Riley shifted, lowering himself fully to the floor from his squat.

He probably realized we would be here a while.

I pulled the shirt closer. "Maybe not. But maybe it is."

"It could be a stain."

I squinted. "You're right. It could be. But why was it left in this box?"

"Maybe so the metal box wouldn't jingle around."

That could be the case. I mean, the shirt had been wrapped around the metal box. "Possibly."

Suddenly, this locked container was even more intriguing.

At first, I'd suspected the possibility of ratty underwear and canned beans.

But now I had a map, a camera, a locked metal box, and a shirt with a weird reddish-brown stain.

As I heard voices in the distance, I quickly stuffed the items back into the banker's box.

I didn't want anyone else to see the metal box or the shirt. Not yet.

Then I remembered the man who'd bid against me.

What if blood *had* stained this shirt? What if the person who'd worn it had been involved with a crime?

My thoughts skittered in a million different directions.

I needed to make sense of this.

But not here.

Suddenly, being out in the open didn't seem like a great idea.

"Gabby . . ." Riley's voice held warning. "What are you thinking?"

"I'm not thinking anything." Maybe that was my problem. I needed to start thinking of *something*.

Riley continued just staring at me, a touch of skepticism in his gaze.

As he did, the voices passed.

Then I heard a single set of footsteps.

Coming toward the unit.

What if it was the man who'd been bidding against me?

What if he knew what was inside this box, and he wanted it back?

That man had wanted this storage unit for some reason—most likely not just to mark something off his bucket list like me.

What if there was more to this storage than I could have ever guessed?

————

I continued to hold my breath until I spotted the owner of the footsteps.

The auctioneer.

He kept walking past.

He appeared to be leaving for the day.

I released the air from my lungs as I realized how I'd been overreacting. Thank goodness.

When I was sure no one was watching, I picked up the camera again and opened a compartment on the side.

I'd halfway expected to see film there.

Instead, the device was digital.

I hit another button, and the SD card popped out from the side.

"Think there's something valuable on that?" Riley raised his eyebrows.

"I've lost all hope that there's anything valuable about this unit."

Despite those words, I took the SD card and shoved it into the pocket of my jeans. Then I placed the camera, metal box, shirt, and the map back into the banker's box, put the lid on, and stood.

I grabbed the box and propped it on my hip as I turned to Riley. "Maybe this was all a bust. But maybe it wasn't."

"What exactly are you going to do with that box?" He nodded at it.

"First, I want to see what's on this SD card. My computer doesn't have a slot for them, but I was just at the drugstore the other day. They have a machine there that prints pictures on demand."

He raised his eyebrows. "Wow . . . you're really intrigued by this, aren't you?"

"Cautiously intrigued."

"You know if it's anything personal, like family photos, you'll need to turn it over to the owners of the storage facility."

"I'm aware." I'd heard at least that much as they'd explained the rules before I got bored and tuned them out. "But maybe it's just generic photographs. Like flowers and trees. If I don't know what's on this, I don't know if I need to turn it over, do I?"

"I suppose that's one way to look at it." He twisted his neck to let me know he didn't totally support my theory.

More than likely, the photos would be nothing. But there was a possibility there was more, and that was a possibility I could *not* dismiss. I had to know.

I started walking toward my van, Riley beside me. As we walked, I kept my eyes open for the man who'd been bidding against me.

I didn't see him.

Still, I felt unusually uneasy.

I glanced at Riley. "I understand if you want nothing to do with this. You don't have to come with me."

"You're my ride."

"True," I muttered. "I *could* drop you off at home. But the drugstore comes first so I might as well stop."

"It *is* on the way." He gave me a side glance. But it wasn't in a way that made him seem truly annoyed. Whenever he seemed annoyed, it was usually in a very "I'm amused" way.

I liked being around Riley. I really did.

In fact, I probably liked being around him a little too much.

I was now a single woman. Chip Parker and I had

just broken up. He was already dating somebody new.

Meanwhile, Riley had been engaged, but now the two of them had broken up. He'd gone on a couple of dates with another woman. Apparently, the two of them hadn't worked out either.

But that didn't mean that Riley and I were a thing. Or even *thinking* about being a thing.

Well, I mean, *I* was thinking about being a thing, but I didn't think he was.

Our relationship was very confusing.

But if I were smart, I'd stay far away from any ideas of romantic relationships. I had a *terrible* track record with men.

Besides, I'd just gone back to school part time so I could finish getting my degree in forensics. I needed to concentrate on my studies.

I hoped to finish college and actually get a more respectable career than being a crime scene cleaner— although I didn't really care what people thought of me in those terms. Being a crime scene cleaner was fascinating. But it wasn't something I wanted to do for the rest of my life either.

I reached my van, opened the back, and placed the banker's box there, where it would be nice and secure.

Then I hopped into the driver's seat, and Riley climbed into my old clunker beside me.

Even though he was a lawyer, he didn't seem embarrassed to be seen in the rundown work van with crime scene cleaning equipment in the back and the vague scent of chemicals lingering on the ripped upholstery.

I'd had visions of buying a new vehicle after selling the treasures I'd purchased sight unseen at auction today.

Some said I had an overactive imagination.

That may be true, but I preferred to think of it as a positive outlook on life.

But life had a twisted sense of humor sometimes.

As I cranked the engine, "Castles in the Sand" by Jimi Hendrix blared from the radio.

Appropriate.

I turned the volume down and shrugged. "Are you sure you don't want me to drop you off before I make any of my other stops?"

I honestly didn't want to get Riley in trouble—not that I was doing anything illegal. If there were personal photos on this SD card, I would turn them in.

And it wasn't necessarily blood on the shirt, so I had nothing to report.

Not yet.

And I had no idea what was inside that metal box.

There were a lot of unknowns, and none of them pointed to the fact I was doing anything wrong.

Me? If I got in trouble . . . sure, I could go to jail. And I didn't want to do that.

But if I got Riley in trouble, he could lose his license to practice law in Virginia. That wouldn't be cool. I cared about Riley too much to endanger his future.

"I'll go with you." Riley offered a decided nod. "So far you haven't done anything illegal."

That was right. Nothing illegal.

Not yet.

Why did that sound an awful lot like I was on the verge of doing so, though?

Maybe Riley knew me better than I thought.

CHAPTER
THREE

A FEW MINUTES LATER, Riley and I pulled into Johnson's Corner Drugstore.

I found the little photo machine I'd seen earlier in the week and quickly read the directions.

Then I inserted the SD card into a small slot and waited for the screen to load.

The machine was taking forever to boot and making me question if this was worth my time or not.

As I waited, I spotted some salt-and-vinegar potato chips and grabbed a bag. This was my favorite brand.

Eating something salty might just be the cure for my remorse over that storage unit. Not a healthy coping mechanism, but my weight hadn't caught up with me.

Not yet.

I looked at the screen again.

The photos still hadn't loaded.

As I turned away from the counter, the hair on my neck rose.

Was someone watching me? That was usually when I got this familiar feeling.

Slowly, I glanced over my shoulder, not wanting to make it too obvious that I was suspicious.

As I did, someone ducked behind the beer and wine aisle.

"Gabby?" Riley turned toward me.

"If you don't mind, print all the pictures on that card for me. Make two copies, for that matter. I need to check something out."

Then I slowly walked toward the aisle.

If someone was watching me, I wanted to know who.

Then I wanted to know why.

———

Just as I reached the beer and wine aisle, I saw the same figure disappear at the end of it.

Whoever had been watching me, he didn't want to be seen.

But that wouldn't deter me.

I picked up my pace, hoping that whoever it was, he wasn't dangerous. And that, even if he was dangerous, he wouldn't pull any nonsense in the middle of a drugstore during the daytime.

Then again, I'd seen crazier things happen.

I cut down a center aisle, determined to somehow catch him.

Just as I peered past shelves full of pain relievers and laxatives, a familiar face caught my eye.

It was the guy from the auction.

The one who'd wanted to buy the same storage space that I had ultimately won.

Had he followed me here?

"Hey!" I called.

As I took off in a jog toward him, he darted away.

I rounded the aisle, but he'd already circled back and headed toward the door.

He sprinted outside.

But before I could follow, a security guard stepped in front of me. "What do you think you're doing?"

I looked down and saw the salt-and-vinegar chips in my hand and frowned. I'd forgotten I'd grabbed them. "I wasn't trying to run out with these."

"That's exactly what it looks like you were doing."

I glanced outside in time to see the man pull away in a bright yellow Trans Am.

Other vehicles blocked me from seeing his license plate number.

But his image—though masked by that hat and those sunglasses—was etched in my mind.

Riley joined me just then. "Everything okay?"

I held up the chips. "I had a mental lapse and nearly ran out the store with these. But I wasn't trying to steal them. I promise."

The security guard gave me a look that made it clear he didn't believe me.

"She has short-term memory issues." Riley patted my back. "We're having a therapist work with her. After the accident she was in . . . it's been difficult, to say the least."

The guard grunted.

I wasn't sure if he believed Riley's explanation or not. But I was kind of impressed that Riley had come up with a cover story so quickly. It didn't seem like him.

Then guilt flooded me.

Church Boy had just lied for me. Was I being a bad influence?

Most definitely, yes. I had no doubt about that.

"Pay and get out of here," the guard finally muttered with a nod to the cashier.

Relief washed through me.

We quickly paid for the chips and then stepped outside.

"What was that about?" Riley whispered as we headed toward my van. "I assumed it was important. That's the only reason I lied."

"I didn't mean for you to do that," I rushed. "But the man from the auction was in the store watching me."

"So you chased him?" Riley's voice rose ever-so-slightly.

"I didn't mean to make him run." I shrugged. "I just wanted to ask him what he was doing."

"That wasn't a good idea, Gabby. Maybe he knows what's inside the metal box. Maybe that's why he wanted to buy that storage unit so badly."

The blood drained from my face at the thought. But I couldn't deny Riley's words. They made sense.

I paused there in the chilly January sunlight and turned toward him. "I'm not 100 percent sure, but I may have stumbled into another mystery."

"And if you did, I'm not at all surprised." Riley gave me another one of his looks.

It was simply adorable.

Then he held up the envelope in his hands. "I have the pictures."

My heart lifted. I'd nearly forgotten about them.

The machine must have started working as soon as I'd walked away.

"Did you look at them yet?" I rushed.

"I figured you would want to."

I grinned. "I do. I really, really do."

RILEY SUGGESTED we grab some coffee nearby and look at the photos. I wasn't about to decline.

I loved spending time with Riley, *and* I loved coffee, so it seemed like a win-win.

We stepped into The Grounds, an old Victorian home that had been turned into a coffeehouse on the first floor and an internet café upstairs. The place was a hodgepodge of tables and chairs squeezed between bright-colored walls filled with abstract art.

Once Riley and I had our coffee and were seated at a corner table, I pulled out the pictures.

And I felt like an investigator about to find the smoking gun as I opened the flap to see what exactly had been on that film.

"Don't get too excited," Riley reminded me as if reading my thoughts. "It could be nothing."

I gave him a pointed look. "Or it could be something."

I opened the paper envelope, trying to avoid the sticky adhesive that held it closed. Then I pulled out the sleeve holding the photos.

I'd gotten two copies.

The first picture showed a tree—a live oak, I thought. They were popular in the area and inter-esting with their horizontal, swooping branches. Another photo was of a bare foot. That one almost looked like it had been taken accidentally.

Then there were wooden legs with blue peeling paint, perhaps belonging to a stool.

Several documents appeared to have been photographed, but the photos were blurry. I couldn't make out any of the words.

I frowned, wishing they were clearer. Whatever was on those documents could be interesting.

Then there was a picture of a hole in the ground. A lone red brick sat beside it, and tall grass concealed the opening. Maybe it was a well. I couldn't be sure.

What I did know was that these photos were random.

Then the last one . . . a gunshot hole through wood shingles.

I stared at that one a moment.

My blood went cold at the sight of it. "This one is kind of creepy."

"I agree." Riley stared at the photo and frowned. "You're *definitely* going to have to give these to the police."

I knew he was right. I couldn't keep these.

But that was okay because I had a spare set.

Was I just being paranoid right now? Or was there more to this?

I glanced up at Riley and took a sip of my vanilla latte before asking, "Am I reading too much into this? Am I trying to find mystery and intrigue where there isn't any?"

I needed to ask the question because I just so happened to find mysteries around every turn. My mind didn't work like other people's. I'd seen too much. Experienced too much.

Riley leaned back, his expression thoughtful. I trusted his opinion. He was smart and a lawyer who'd also seen some of the worst sides of society.

"I definitely think you may have stumbled onto something—especially based on that last photo," he finally said.

On a whim, I rushed toward the barista, Sharon, who just happened to also be a friend. "Do you have a screwdriver or paperclip I could borrow?"

"I have both." She eyed me curiously before pushing her pink hair out of her eyes.

"Can I borrow both?"

She raised a pierced eyebrow. "Of course."

I was thankful Sharon didn't ask too many questions. She disappeared into the back office, only to return a moment later with the items I'd requested.

I needed to see what was inside that locked metal box.

Riley followed me outside to my van.

I opened the back door to retrieve the four-hundred-dollar banker's box.

As I did, the entire container tumbled to the ground. It had obviously shifted as I'd been driving.

The contents poured out.

As they did, the metal box hit the asphalt, and the lock gave.

The top popped open.

And a gun bounced out.

―――――

I sucked in a breath when I saw the weapon.

A gun.

There had been *a gun* inside that metal box.

I left it on the ground, staring at it a moment.

Until I heard voices nearby.

I grabbed the possibly blood-sprayed shirt and used the corner of it to pick up the gun. I placed the weapon in the back of my van before glancing around.

No one could see this.

No one appeared to be watching, not even the man from the auction.

But I needed to be careful.

"Talk about a twist I didn't see coming," I muttered as I stared at the gun. It had bits of dried dirt on it, almost as if it had been buried at some point.

Strange.

"What's the protocol for this?" Riley asked. "Don't you need to report any weapons to the police?"

"Why would I want to do that?"

"Because the auctioneer at the storage facility said anyone who finds a gun in their unit has to turn it in."

"Oh, I wasn't listening. So that doesn't count."

"Okay then. How about because . . . maybe it was stolen. Or used in a crime."

"What are the odds?" I brushed his theory off.

"Considering you're involved . . . ." He tilted his head to the side and sighed. "They're pretty good."

I kind of had to agree with him, but I didn't. Not outwardly, at least.

Because if I agreed with him, then he was going to try to convince me to take this right down to the police station.

And I wasn't ready to do that yet.

Instead, my thoughts continued to race.

I remembered the guy who'd been bidding against me. Remembered seeing him again at the drugstore.

"What if he was the killer?" The question escaped from my lips, even though I had planned to keep it simply in my head.

"So now there's been a murder?"

"A photo of a bullet hole. A gun. A bloody shirt. I'd say the chances are pretty good this involves a dead person."

Riley leaned against my van, his arms crossed. "So the guy who bid against you is a killer?"

"Why else would he have followed us earlier?"

"That's a good question. There *was* something suspicious about him. Maybe he knows something."

My thoughts continued to race. "But if he was a killer and he knew evidence to a murder was in that storage unit, why wouldn't he just pay to renew the lease on it rather than going through all this trouble?"

"That is also an excellent question, one you'd have to figure out if you were investigating. But you're not . . . because you're going to the police and turning everything in . . . right?"

I shrugged noncommittally. Now that I'd given everything a second to sink in, my thoughts felt clearer. "That would be the only smart thing to do."

"It would be more than smart, it would be *responsible*."

Riley's words hit me with conviction—which I was sure was what he had meant to do.

But I didn't want to be convicted right now. I wanted to be left to my own devices so I could investigate freely without any guilt.

It didn't look like that was going to happen.

Guilt was overrated anyway.

But still . . .

I picked up my phone and opened my contacts.

I didn't want to do this.

But I hit Parker's number.

I needed to tell someone what had happened, and my ex—a detective with the Norfolk PD—seemed like the best choice.

CHAPTER
FIVE

PARKER HAD SOUNDED IRRITATED, just as I'd expected. Something about me *always* irritated him. It seemed to be my superpower when he was around.

Sometimes I still couldn't believe I'd dated the man. He was handsome, and that had drawn me in. He was also a detective, which had also intrigued me.

But that was really where our compatibility and attraction ended.

Like I said, I had a terrible history when it came to dating.

Which was why I should stay single indefinitely.

Parker had instructed Riley and me to go back to my apartment, and he'd said he would meet us there. So that's what we did.

Part of me didn't expect Riley to stick around.

I'd given him ample opportunity to go back to his own apartment and resume his day as he pleased— perhaps resume in a way that didn't involve crime or snooping. But he'd insisted on staying.

I wasn't sure if it was because he was curious or if he was concerned how I'd handle turning this information over. Either way, Parker might want to talk to Riley since he was with me when I found the weapon.

I'd barely been in my apartment long enough to place my purse and the box on my coffee table and to light an apple-scented candle when I heard a knock at my door.

That was fast.

I quickly did a couple more things before I headed toward the door, just as I heard another rapid —impatient—knock.

Riley had already disappeared into the bathroom, leaving me alone to face Parker.

I opened the front door, not sure exactly how I'd feel upon seeing my ex.

The man looked like Brad Pitt—Brad Pitt back when he was cute. Not that he wasn't cute anymore. He was. But Parker was in his early thirties, and his looks were practically flawless. He was well aware of that fact.

Parker leaned against the doorframe as he waited for me to answer. He wore jeans and a thick navy-blue sweater that made me wonder if he was officially working today or if I'd caught him on his day off.

"Gabby, Gabby, Gabby . . ." He clicked his tongue as if chiding me. "What have you gotten yourself into now?"

I extended my hand behind me to invite him inside. "Good to see you too, Parker. How is Charlie?"

"She's great." Was that a flash of guilt in his gaze?

I knew Parker pretty much had been dating Charlie even before the two of us had officially broken up. I mean, maybe it was an unofficial type of dating. But they'd definitely had feelings for each other and were flirting.

But whatever. Better to see the light earlier rather than later.

"Where is this box?" He raised his eyebrows as he stepped inside.

"If I give it to you, do you think there's any way I can get my money back for buying the storage unit? Because my only reason for buying it was to recoup the money by selling what was inside."

His gaze darkened. "You can't sell items that may have potentially been used in a crime."

"You don't know these things were used in a crime. Someone could have simply left their gun in the unit for safekeeping."

Riley emerged from the bathroom in time to hear my statement. He looked at me with raised eyebrows. Sure, we'd just been talking about there being a murder involved. But Parker didn't need to know that.

"People don't generally leave guns places."

"Maybe the guy died."

Parker gave me an impatient look and tapped his foot.

Before he could offer a smart retort, he spotted Riley standing in my kitchen.

Instantly, Parker stiffened.

"Riley." He nodded, his playfulness disappearing.

"Parker." Riley sounded equally stiff.

As the two men observed each other a moment, the air itself seemed to be cringing with awkwardness.

It wasn't as if Riley had feelings for me. And it wasn't as if Parker had feelings for me either, for that matter. So I wasn't sure why the two guys were having a face-off as if trying to determine whose territory I was.

Because I was no one's territory.

I cleared my throat and crossed my arms.

"There's the box." I nodded toward the table.

Parker pulled some latex gloves from his pocket and slipped them on. Then he walked toward the banker's box and took off the lid.

"Let's see what's inside," he muttered.

Speaking of being territorial . . . I was feeling pretty territorial about that box. I didn't really want Parker messing with it. Or anyone with the police.

You know those games people could order online? The ones that were mysteries in a box where you and your friends got together to try to figure out what really happened?

Well, this felt like my real-life version of that.

I had just dived into the clues, and now someone was taking the game away.

That annoyed me to no end.

But I wasn't going to sit back and let just anyone tell me what I could and couldn't do.

Especially not Parker.

———

Despite my annoyance, I stood where I was, shoving my hands into the pockets of my jeans so I wouldn't be tempted to touch anything off-limits.

"So tell me again what happened." Parker started as he observed the camera.

I went through the spiel with him again. I reminded him that before I'd discovered the gun, I found the camera and had the pictures developed.

What he didn't know was that I had two sets of the pictures printed. One set was now safely tucked in my purse. I'd also taken a picture of the map while Riley had run into the bathroom earlier.

At least I had access to those things. Parker would take the shirt and gun, and that was fine with me. I couldn't test the shirt for blood—that would be unwise. And I was no weapons expert, so I wouldn't be able to test the gun myself.

Parker checked to make sure the gun wasn't loaded and then studied the slide, probably looking at the serial number.

"I'll run this and see if it's tied to any robberies." He put it down on the table.

"Or murders." I muttered. "Check those too."

He glanced up at me, his eyes narrowing. "Any idea how long it's been since that storage unit was paid for?"

"The storage unit facility owner didn't give out any personal details. Do you want me to try to find out?"

"No. Absolutely not."

I shrugged. "Just trying to help."

"The best way you can try to help is by not trying to help."

"Ouch." Not really. I'd expected his words and figured he'd say something jerky. "You'll have to talk to the owner of the storage facility. I didn't ask that many questions."

"Don't worry. I will. Anything else you can tell me, Nancy Drew?"

I let out a sigh, my resolve to be polite slipping and my irritation showing. "Not really."

Parker picked up the pictures and glanced at me. "You went ahead and had them developed, huh?"

"I didn't know what was on them."

"But you had to know they'd be a personal effect."

I shrugged innocently. "I'm handing the photos over now. Besides, you know me. I wasn't paying attention to all the rules."

"You never do." He did a half eye roll.

I wanted to argue, but I couldn't. Parker was right.

I hated rules.

He let out a grunt and then began flipping through the pictures, letting out even more grunts as he did so.

I watched his expression carefully, curious about his thoughts on the photos.

Because I knew for certain that whatever I'd stumbled into was serious.

Very serious.

Maybe even *deadly* serious.

CHAPTER SIX

"DO you recognize anything in the photos?" I asked after several minutes of silence.

Parker had been a detective in the area for a while. Maybe something in one of those photos had stirred a memory of a crime.

But if those photos were from a crime, why would the killer save them? Wouldn't the killer know the pictures could possibly incriminate him one day?

Maybe the killer had hidden the evidence in the storage facility in order to keep it safe. But then something had happened to this person.

A chill washed through me at the thought.

I wanted to believe that couldn't be true.

But I knew it could be.

"No, I don't recognize anything." Parker frowned

as he spoke, yet his gaze was intense as he studied them with curiosity.

I glanced over and saw Riley studying my expression. He was wondering what I was thinking, wasn't he?

I couldn't blame him. I had some crazy ideas float through my head sometimes. Then again, my brain cells did really weird things sometimes. Things like coming up with random song lyrics. Diving in when I should be running away. Pressing harder when I should be easing off.

Parker stuck everything back in the banker's box, placed the lid on it, and then grabbed it. "I'm going to need to take these with me and run some tests."

"Let me know what you find out." I made the statement knowing good and well that he would not be doing that.

The look he gave me confirmed it. "Yeah, right."

"I'm the one who's out four hundred dollars right now," I reminded him with a frown.

Really, I was only mad at myself. I should have known better. But Parker was a good scapegoat. He, if anyone, deserved it.

Then again, I was glad I didn't get everything I deserved.

He didn't say anything.

That was probably because Parker didn't really

care about being in debt—not if it meant living the lifestyle he wanted. One day, I figured it would all catch up with him.

But that day hadn't come yet.

With one more glance, he was out the door. I closed it behind him and then leaned against it.

What now?

Could I let this go and return to my regularly scheduled Saturday night?

That was doubtful. So, so doubtful.

"That feels anti-climactic," I finally murmured after Parker was gone.

Riley stepped closer, and I caught a whiff of his woodsy scent. I tried not to lean into it—because that would be weird. Really weird. But man, did I want to.

"What are you thinking?" He studied my expression. "Don't say nothing. I can read it on you."

There was no need for me to hold my thoughts inside. Besides, I was dying to tell someone.

I blurted my theory that the killer had hidden evidence in the storage unit.

To my surprise, Riley didn't discount it.

Not that he usually discounted me. Maybe I was

programmed to think that way after dating Parker. I was pretty sure Parker's goal in life had been to make me feel small.

For a while, it had worked.

"Your idea has a lot of merit," he murmured.

I let out a long breath, relieved at his words. I wasn't sure why I wanted his approval so much, but I did.

I supposed I had him on a pedestal. I knew it was dangerous, but that's where he was.

I turned my thoughts back to the subject at hand and let out a sigh. "But I guess I'll forget about it. I'll move on and let the police do their thing."

"You and I both know that's not going to happen. Once you get your hands on something, you have a hard time letting go. Mysteries are to you like flypaper is to a . . ."

"Fly?"

He shrugged. "Maybe not the best analogy. But, yes. You're drawn to them."

"And then I get stuck and nearly die." Maybe his analogy wasn't that far off after all. "Are you saying I should investigate?"

"I'm saying that I know whatever I say, you're going to investigate anyway. So I might as well be with you when you do it. Safety in numbers and all, you know?"

My heart skipped a beat. His words were like magic to my ears.

"I was hoping you might say that." I grinned and pulled out my phone. "I took a picture of that map."

Riley's eyes widened. "When did you do that?"

"When you were in the bathroom. I didn't think you'd approve, so I was trying to not fall into the wrath of your judgment."

"The wrath of my judgment?" He tilted his head as if offended.

"Maybe an overstatement. But I was avoiding conflict."

He gave me another look before nodding at my phone. "Let's see that map."

More excitement pulsed through me as I found the picture and enlarged it.

Two different addresses had been marked.

"Which one should we start with?" Riley asked.

"I say we start with this one." I pointed to the location closest to us.

The address was a neighborhood probably ten minutes away, in an area of town that was fairly rundown and crime-ridden.

"Then let's start there," he murmured.

I felt as giddy as a girly girl being crowned with a fake tiara as I grabbed my purse, and we left.

CHAPTER
SEVEN

RILEY HAD INSISTED ON DRIVING, and I didn't try to stop him. Besides, I wanted to look at these pictures again. I wanted to study them and see if I could find any clues the second time around.

Riley had already programmed the address into the GPS of his car, so I didn't have to help with directions. That meant I could give my full attention to the photos.

I glanced at the stack in my hands and frowned.

They each seemed so abstract. A stool. A tree. A well.

A bare foot. A shingle with a bullet hole. Blurry documents.

Was the person who'd taken them a photographer in training? Were these still photos?

Or did they indicate something sinister?

I had no idea.

Maybe they weren't significant at all. Maybe none of this was.

This could be a complete wild goose chase. It wouldn't be my first one.

Finally, we pulled in front of an old two-story house that had probably been beautiful at one time. But not any longer.

Now the white paint was peeling, the porch was sagging, and one of the windows was broken. Not only that, but the grass hadn't been cut in ages . . . probably since Angry Birds was popular.

An orange notice from the city had been placed on the front door, probably condemning the place.

"It doesn't look like anyone's lived here in a very long time," I murmured.

"What do you want to do?" Riley stared at the structure, a strange frown on his face, almost as if this house made him feel uneasy.

"I want a better look. Maybe read the sign on the door and see it says what I think it does. I'm not sure how much information we're going to get here. But I'd like to look this address up and see who lived here at one time."

He nodded. "I figured you'd say that. You should probably look the information up later. You're going to have to make this a quick visit. If I'm guessing right, the police will be here before too long. The last thing you want is for Parker to find you snooping."

Riley's words made me tense. He was absolutely correct. I did *not* want Parker to find me here right now. I didn't want to listen to one of his demeaning lectures.

Instead, I placed my hand on the door handle. "Let's go."

"Wait . . ."

I froze and looked at Riley, wondering if he knew something I didn't.

"I want to pull around the corner . . . just in case someone else shows up," he told me. "We don't want to be too obvious."

A slow grin spread across my face. "I like the way you think."

"Really? Because the way I think is starting to scare me."

"Isn't it great?"

He gave me a look. "That isn't exactly what I'd call it."

Then he pulled away, thinking exactly like a detective.

I was so proud.

———

Riley started to walk toward the front of the house with me when he paused. "Maybe I should stay here as a lookout instead."

I nodded, impressed with his thought process. "Good idea. If you see Parker—or anyone else suspicious—coming my way, please let me know."

He nodded and then took his place on the sidewalk.

As he did, I rushed toward the rickety front porch.

When I got there, I paused. My gaze instantly went to a little blue wooden milk stool near the front door.

I blinked several times as I stared at the numerous scratches, dents, and scrapes on its surface.

I'd seen this before.

It had been in one of the photos I'd had printed. I was certain of it.

My heart pounded harder. Just what kind of significance did this house have exactly?

I wasn't sure.

I picked up the stool and examined it, but it didn't appear to be anything special.

Then my eyes narrowed as I stared at the porch floorboards beneath it.

There were some strange cuts in them.

Using my fingernails, I tried to pry one of the boards up.

It lifted more easily than I'd anticipated.

Right beneath it was a small compartment—maybe one where people left shoes to store them out of the way. I'd seen something like this once beneath a welcome mat and had thought the idea was brilliant.

There was nothing inside it now, but this would be the perfect place to hide something.

Was that what the photographer had discovered? Had something been in this cubby?

Maybe.

Next, I glanced up at the orange sign on the door. It was just as I thought. The place had been condemned—and rightfully so. The floorboards on the porch squeaked and bent under my weight, and I feared that at any moment I might fall through.

Despite that, I went to the window and peered inside, hoping to catch a glimpse of the interior of the house.

Dirt covered the glass, and a thick curtain concealed most of the view. What I could see wasn't significant. A living room with fairly outdated furniture.

I hurried down the steps and toward the back-yard. The last thing I needed was for a neighbor to call the police on me. It had happened before, so it was a distinct possibility.

I paused by a live oak in the corner. Its long, drooping branches hung near the ground in a glorious display.

A tree had been in one of the photos also. Was it this tree?

If so, how would it be significant?

I wasn't sure.

I glanced back at the house, searching for that bullet hole from the picture.

I didn't see anything. I didn't even think the siding matched, so that was a dead end.

There was nothing else of note in the backyard except the overgrown grass. There were no swings or playsets or even a patio table.

But as I stood there, I felt an immense sense that something bad had happened here. I wasn't usually one to give a lot of significance to premonitions. But I couldn't shake the feeling I had right now.

A stick cracked in the distance, and my spine stiffened.

Without turning my head, I glanced around, looking for the source of the noise.

A chain-link fence surrounded the place. I hated to say it, but the neighbors on either side didn't take much better care of their yards. They were overgrown with lots of shrubs and trees with low branches that concealed this backyard.

I continued to glance around, hoping for a sign of what had made the noise.

That's when I saw someone hiding behind a bush on the other side of the fence.

My entire body went still.

CHAPTER
EIGHT

AT ONCE, the man realized I'd spotted him.

He jumped to his feet.

It was the same guy from earlier, wasn't it?

As the man took off into a run, I took three steps toward him.

I wasn't sure what I thought I would do if I caught him. Tackle him? Put him in a choke hold? Pray he tripped and hit his head to subdue him until police arrived?

I wasn't sure, but as it turns out it didn't matter anyway.

I hadn't made it very far when Riley called my name.

I paused and glanced back toward the house.

Riley motioned to me from the front yard.

"Gabby. We have to go. I see Parker's car at the end of the street. He's coming this way."

I stared at the fleeing figure for one more moment.

I really wanted to catch that guy and find out what his connection was to this case.

To find out if maybe he was a killer and if that gun had belonged to him.

But that could also be a very bad idea—especially if he was armed.

"Gabby . . ." Riley called again.

I looked away from the guy and back at Riley. With a nod, I jogged toward him.

We cut through the corner of the neighbor's lawn to make it to his car.

We jumped in and pulled away. I looked in the sideview mirror in time to see Parker pull to a stop in front of the house.

I wondered if he'd go inside. If he'd discover something I hadn't.

It didn't matter. Even if Parker did, it wasn't as if he'd share that information with me.

But I'd definitely stumbled into something here. Maybe even something big.

There was no way I was going to give up until I had some answers.

"So . . . what happened back there?" Riley asked as he turned in the opposite direction of Parker.

I told him about the milk stool and the tree that could've been from the photos. Then I told him about the man hiding in the bushes.

He drew in a short breath. "I don't like the sound of that."

"The guy didn't appear to want to hurt me. He had the opportunity and didn't take it. But he's definitely watching me for some reason."

"He must have known that evidence was in that storage unit and that's why he wanted to buy it. Now he's trying to see what you're doing with everything you found inside."

"But if the guy who's following me is the owner of the gun or if he had something to do with a crime of some sort, why bid on this storage unit instead of simply breaking in and taking what he wanted? I mean, let's say a murder happened. I would think someone who was willing to commit murder would also be willing to break into a storage unit."

Riley clicked his tongue. "I can't deny that. I'm not sure what's going on here, but you raise a good point." He continued down the road. "What now?"

"I want to do research on that house and see if there are any news articles connected to it."

"Good idea. How about if we order some Chinese and see what we can find out?"

I tried to hide my smile. But I loved the thought of Riley and I working together on this. Really, investigating these things was so much more fun when you had someone doing it with you.

Especially when I had Riley doing it with me.

Yes, I had it bad. I hoped Riley couldn't see it on my face.

"That sounds like a plan," I said, careful to keep my voice even and not sound too thrilled to be working with him.

But for the rest of the ride home, my thoughts continued to race.

CHAPTER
NINE

AS SOON AS Riley and I got back to our apartment complex and stepped inside, my best friend, Sierra Nakamura, stepped out from her downstairs apartment.

When she did, one of her cats sashayed past her and into the common area near the stairs. The scent of incense and essential oils floated out along with the sounds of Whales at Twilight.

Yes, Whales at Twilight. I only knew what it was called because Sierra talked all the time about her noise machine and the many sounds she could play on it. She was really into white noise and the sounds of nature—anything to help her find her zen.

The animal rights activist was unique, to say the least. I didn't always agree with her methods, but I loved her as a person. She'd been a faithful friend.

"What's going on?" Sierra squinted as she looked at me then Riley as if sensing something had happened. "You've been gone all day. How did the auction go?"

Riley and I glanced at each other.

"We'll have to fill you in," I finally said. "Do you want to come eat some Chinese food with us?"

"I'd love to. But only if you order from somewhere I can get sweet and sour tofu."

We agreed.

Ten minutes later, she joined us in my apartment.

I was itching to grab my laptop and start doing research. But first, I had to clear off my kitchen table, which I had covered with samples of blood spatter I was studying for one of my classes. Then I had to do some dishes so we'd have something to eat on and quickly straighten my bathroom also.

To say I hadn't been expecting guests would be an understatement. Although I spent my time cleaning other people's houses and scrubbing the blood and gore from them, my own apartment often suffered. Go figure.

I assumed Riley was the type who'd want to be with someone neat, tidy, and organized. In other words, someone not like me.

Someone who was more like his ex-fiancée,

Veronica. The woman had been beautiful, wealthy, and entirely put together.

Then there was Amy, the other girl Riley had gone on a couple dates with. Surprisingly, she wasn't like Veronica. Instead, she'd been friendly and steady. She was on the quieter side, worked for social services, and she'd grown up in church.

Either way, neither of those women were like me. Which meant I wasn't Riley's type at all.

Finally, the food was delivered, and we spread it across the center of my secondhand kitchen table. It was straight from the seventies. But it worked.

Once our plates were full, I grabbed my computer and typed with one hand, while eating General Tso's chicken with my chopsticks in the other.

I typed in the address Riley and I had visited. As I waited for the results to fill the page, I wondered if Parker was still at that house. If he'd discovered anything.

And I wondered who that man was who'd been watching me.

"So . . ." I glanced at Riley. "We had to sign in when we went to that auction. I'm sure that the guy bidding against us for the storage unit had to sign in also. Do you think the owner of the storage company would let us know his name?"

Riley scrunched his face skeptically. "Probably

not. But even if he did, my gut feeling is that this guy probably didn't use his real name."

A frown tugged at my lips. He was right. If the guy had used his real name, then he wasn't very smart. And if he wasn't very smart, then he would probably get caught very soon by Parker.

But I did store that idea away for later use just in case none of our other leads panned out. It could be worth following up on.

For now, I needed to find out the history of this house.

It had to be significant. I just needed to know why.

———

It didn't take very long for the address to pop up.

"You guys . . ." I leaned closer to the screen, unable to believe my eyes. "How did we not know about this?"

"Know about what?" Riley also leaned closer.

"A man was killed at that house two years ago." I vaguely remembered hearing about the death now that more details were coming to light. I'd been a crime scene cleaner back then, but I usually only worked inside homes—not in backyards, which was where this guy had been killed.

"What?" Sierra pushed her glasses up higher on her nose.

We'd already filled her in on the events that had happened today, so she was up to speed on things. Having her here was actually good. She was as smart as a whip. Maybe she'd see something we didn't.

"This guy who was shot . . . his name was Billy O'Brien . . . he was twenty-two. At first, investigators thought he'd taken his own life. However, upon further investigation, they determined the angle of the bullet didn't match what could be suicide. The gun would have been at too high an angle for him to hold the gun like that."

I stared at the picture of Billy. He was thin and tall with shaggy brown hair. He had some acne scarring on his cheeks and heavy eyebrows. But, in the photo, he was smiling as he stood in front of an old, beat-up Buick with his thumbs raised.

"What else does it say?" Riley shifted as he listened, his total attention on me.

I averted my gaze from the pictures. "The police then moved on to the theory that maybe he was in the wrong place at the wrong time. The neighborhood has a lot of drug activity, so investigators thought maybe he wandered into the backyard, not realizing a deal was going down."

"Interesting theory. I guess they never proved it was true?"

"No, they didn't." I kept reading. "Apparently, this guy Billy had no relatives other than a stepsister named Trudy. He also had no known enemies. He worked as a mechanic, and his friends described him as laid-back and quiet."

"What about the murder weapon?" Riley asked.

"According to this, the police believed it was a Smith and Wesson 9 mm."

Riley's eyes narrowed. "What . . . kind of gun was that again in the metal box?"

"A Smith and Wesson 9 mm." The words left my lips with a vague tinge of triumph.

We were onto something here. I was certain of it. That fact seemed to prove it.

"Was anyone ever arrested?" Sierra expertly picked up a piece of broccoli with her chopsticks and popped it in her mouth as she waited for the answer.

"There's one man listed as a person of interest," I told them. "Bruce Clemmons. Apparently, the police did not have enough evidence to hold him. He was, however, caught using Billy's credit card. He said he found it on the sidewalk and capitalized on the opportunity. Otherwise, there was no known connection between the men."

"What sidewalk did he claim to find this credit

card on?" Riley scooped some more shrimp fried rice onto his plate.

I scanned the rest of the article. "It looks like it was . . . near Billy's work."

Riley nodded. "Interesting. Did Billy ever report it missing?"

"I don't see any mention of that, so I'm going to assume no."

"Do any of the articles have a picture of the man?" Riley asked.

I clicked off that article onto a new one, hoping to discover some updated information.

Finally, I found a photo of Bruce and clicked on the image to enlarge it.

I turned the laptop so Sierra and Riley could also see. The man had ginger-colored hair and a thick ginger beard.

"This is Bruce," I told them. "And he is *not* the man who was following us today."

"So who was that man?" Sierra shrugged. "Why would he be following you? What exactly is his connection?"

"And if the guy who's following us is the killer, I simply can't imagine why he would keep that evidence, knowing it could be found one day and incriminate him," Riley added. "Most criminals would destroy it rather than risk it being found—like what happened today."

He made an excellent point.

There was obviously a lot going on here, more than we could fully understand.

Riley was in full-on lawyer mode, his gaze focused and assessing. "What about that second location that was marked on the map?"

I pulled it up on my phone and typed the address into my computer.

I frowned at the results. "It's a feed and seed store."

"That's . . . unexpected." Riley raised his eyebrows.

"It sure is." I clicked on a link to the location. "And . . . it closed thirty minutes ago, so we can't head there now."

I frowned, which was silly. Billy had been murdered two years ago. I wasn't sure why I wanted immediate answers. Maybe I was impatient like that.

But yes, I'd wanted to head there after dinner.

"When does it open tomorrow?" Riley leaned closer to see my screen.

"Not until one."

"Perfect. After church and lunch, I'm game for heading out there to see what we can find out, if you are."

That's right. *Perfect.*

I needed to look at the situation like that.

And I needed to remember that Riley was offering to help me right now. Win, win, win!

I smiled and picked up another piece of my chicken. "You're right. That sounds like a *perfect* plan."

JUST AS WE HAD DISCUSSED, Riley and I went to church together the next morning.

The congregation he attended met in a high school, and the fearless leader of the flock was a man I affectionately called Pastor Shaggy. His real name was Randy, but he looked exactly like Shaggy from Scooby-Doo, thus the nickname.

Six months ago, I hadn't wanted anything to do with church. But now the idea was beginning to grow on me. That was partly because Riley didn't shush me when I asked him the hard questions. There was still so much about God that I struggled to understand.

Most of those ideas had been shaped and formed when I was a child. My younger brother, Timmy, had been kidnapped while I was watching him. To this day, we didn't know what happened to him.

That had set off a spiral of heartache for me and my family. My dad had started drinking. He still struggled with alcohol to this day.

I'd known during those moments that if there was a God that He didn't love me. That He was like a dad who picked and chose His favorite children—some He gave blessings to and others He shunned.

I was one of the ones He shunned.

Coming to church with Riley was beginning to change my perspective. However, Riley constantly reminded me that I couldn't put my faith in the people of the church either. My faith had to be in God alone. He said that people I met at church were mostly good people, but they still had problems. They were still imperfect. They were still going to let me down.

Even him.

Part of me wanted to think that Riley could never let me down. But that wasn't true. I already knew that. Because he'd already broken my heart when I thought he'd liked me only to have his fiancée show up. Or former fiancée.

It was a long, complicated story.

I tried to tell myself it didn't matter or make a difference. But I knew that it did.

I set those thoughts aside as the church service ended. I glanced at the time and saw it was only 11:30.

"What do you say we go to that Mexican restaurant we like?" Riley proposed.

Based on the grin I felt spreading across my face, I knew there was no hiding just how happy his suggestion made me. "That sounds perfect."

By the time we finished eating, the feed and seed store would be open. I couldn't wait to see what we might find out there.

But if that didn't work out and we didn't find any new evidence there, then I already had a list of other things we could do to find the information we might need.

On that list, as a last resort, was talking to Parker.

———

The taste of spicy salsa and the salty tortilla chips still lingered in my mouth as we pulled up to Hank's Feed and Seed. The store was located in Norfolk and had apparently opened back when the area had been more rural. Urban garden enthusiasts still shopped there, however.

Riley and I stared at the place a moment before getting out.

"What do you think?" I asked. "Should we come up with a cover story to try to get information out of them? Or should we just be direct about why we're here?"

"In this case, I feel like being direct is the best idea. I don't see any reason why we'd need a cover story in this situation." Riley shrugged.

I don't know why I felt disappointed at his words. I hadn't realized that I liked cover stories and acting so much until just this moment. Maybe this came from reading too many Nancy Drew books as a child.

"Okay then. We go with the truth." I grabbed the handle of the car door and opened it.

A chilly January breeze swept over me, and I pulled my coat closer. Despite the weather, I'd worn flip-flops. I liked them that much. But right now, my toes were cold. I'd never admit it if anyone asked, however.

When we stepped inside, the scent of fertilizer and grass seed surrounded me. I couldn't be sure those were the *exact* smells, but that was what I imagined them to be, at least.

A man stood behind the counter. Maybe boy would be a better description. He appeared to still be in high school, which meant he wouldn't be ideal to speak with. I guessed him to be maybe seventeen, which would have made him fifteen around the time of the murder.

"We need to find somebody else to talk to."

But before I could peruse the store, the teen spotted us and offered a friendly smile. I had a feeling he was the type of guy who didn't know a stranger.

"Welcome to Hank's Feed and Seed. Can I help you with something?" He grinned at both of us.

"Is there anyone else working who can help us?" I pressed my lips shut as soon as the question escaped. The words had come out wrong.

Riley gave me a look. "What she means is that we're looking for someone who may have worked here two years ago. Is there anyone here right now who might fit that description?"

"Two years ago?" He tapped his lips. "I can't say for sure because I have only worked here three months myself. But if I had to guess, you should talk to Grandpa Lee."

"Where can we find Grandpa Lee?" Riley asked.

"He's right over there near the mealworms."

Riley and I started toward the man.

"Thanks for correcting me back there," I told Riley quietly. "I didn't exactly mean for my words to sound the way that they did."

"It's all right. I just hope we can find some answers."

We paused beside a man who appeared to be in his seventies. He was tall and thin with a slight hunch. He had stark white hair that was thick on the side and thin on the top. His scratchy voice sounded friendly and knowledgeable.

As soon as he wrapped up his conversation with a customer discussing how to best feed mealworms to birds, he turned to us.

He held a brand-new shovel in his hands, and I suspected he'd been on his way to place it with the others on the wall behind him when a customer had stopped him.

The man grinned at us. "How can I help you two? Looking for some feed for your chickens?"

That would have been so much fun to play off of. Riley and I as the farmer types? That would be a sitcom in the making.

I resisted the urge to sing "Do the Funky Chicken" and dance along. *That* was how my mind worked.

"Actually, I have a rather strange question," I started. Maybe I should've thought this part through a little bit more because this was going to sound totally random. Based on my earlier track record, who knew how the words were going to be leaving my lips right now.

"Oh, I like helping people, so what do you need?"

"I don't want to over explain," I started, feeling that would be a good lead-in. "However, I was wondering if anyone who ever worked here was associated with Billy O'Brien?"

Lee blinked. "Who?"

"Billy O'Brien," I repeated. "He lived in Norfolk, and he was killed two years ago. You may have heard about his story on the news."

Lee shifted, and I was all too aware of the shovel he was leaning on like a cane. All he had to do was lift that tool and swing . . . Riley and I wouldn't stand a chance.

The thought wasn't comforting.

I waited for his reaction and prayed talking to him wasn't a mistake.

ELEVEN

"BILLY O'BRIEN . . ." Lee shook his head. "I can't say that name rings any bells. Why are you asking?"

I heard his question, but I couldn't pull my gaze away from that shovel long enough to answer him.

"Some new evidence has been uncovered." Riley seemed to sense my unease and stepped in. "Your store location was marked on a map found correlating to the investigation into his death."

Did I mention I was so glad Riley was with me? He always seemed to know when I needed him most.

"And who are you both?" Lee glanced between the two of us, as if trying to figure out if this was some type of trap. A touch of his friendliness disappeared, replaced with suspicion.

I couldn't blame him. I'd be the same way.

"My apologies. I'm Riley Thomas, an attorney.

Some information has recently been uncovered, and my colleague and I are trying to ascertain whether it's sufficient to reopen the case."

I tried not to raise my eyebrows. But I was surprised at how easily Riley had come up with that cover story. And I was also a little shocked that he hadn't told the complete truth.

Again.

However, there was *a lot* of truth to his words. Even though we hadn't talked to Parker, I felt certain if enough evidence emerged that new life could be brought to the case.

"I see." Lee nodded slowly and thoughtfully, as if trying to come up with some memories. "I can't recall that name in particular. I have no idea why our store would be mentioned in any evidence concerning that case."

"Is there anyone else who worked here two years ago who might have an idea?" I asked.

Lee puckered his lips in a thoughtful frown. "We're a small family-run business. My father started this place when I was only ten years old, and we've kept it in the family ever since. That's my grandson working over there at the register now. I've got to say, I'm probably your best bet in finding out information, though my wife might recall something."

"Is she around?" Riley asked.

Lee frowned. "Unfortunately, she's not well. But if she has a good day, I'll ask her if she remembers anything. Why don't you leave me your card?"

Riley nodded and pulled a business card from his pocket. "We'd appreciate that. Here you go."

With that conversation done, Riley and I started toward the exit.

But I couldn't deny the disappointment pressing into me.

If Lee didn't have any answers, then this whole lead would be a dead end. How else would we figure out the connection between this place and the crime?

I didn't have any great ideas.

But it couldn't be a coincidence that this location was marked and left with the gun and photos.

It just couldn't be.

———

It was 1:30 when Riley and I climbed back into his car.

We sat there a moment.

My thoughts still raced as I tried to calculate what to do next.

"So . . . ?" Riley glanced at me.

A decision solidified in my mind. "If you don't

mind, I'd like to call Parker and see if he'll share any information with me."

Riley shoved his eyebrows together as if skeptical. "Do you think that he will?"

"No, not at all. But I thought it could be worth a shot."

His expression softened, and he shrugged. "Then you might as well give it the old college try."

I quickly dialed Parker's number, and he answered on the first ring, sounding just as cranky and annoyed as ever.

"Yes?" That was his greeting for me.

He knew me well enough to know why I was calling.

"How's it going?" I tried to sound friendly and make some small talk.

I was still working on not blurting out the first thing that came to mind. But those skills were still in progress.

"Why don't you just ask me whatever you want to ask?" Parker muttered. "No need to draw this out any longer than necessary."

"What makes you think that's why I called?" I made sure I sounded slightly offended.

He let out a sigh so loud Lee could probably hear it inside the store. "I don't know . . . how about the fact that one of the neighbors reported seeing a girl with curly red hair outside the property where Billy O'Brien was murdered—right before we arrived to investigate yesterday."

"What?" Drats! I didn't think anyone had seen me other than the man hiding in the bushes.

That would have been too easy, I supposed.

Despite myself, I asked, "Did you find anything there?"

"You know I'm not supposed to speak about these things."

I heard someone in the background—a feminine voice.

Parker was with Charlie right now, wasn't he?

I didn't really have any hard feelings, however. Our breakup was for the best. Actually, I kind of felt bad for Charlie because Parker may look like Prince Charming, but he acted more like Gaston from *Beauty and the Beast*. Our whole relationship had been a dumpster fire.

Despite that, Charlie, who was also a detective, could certainly handle herself in delicate situations.

"I'm going to have to assume that you didn't find anything," I continued. "But that you *did* notice that the milk stool and the tree in the backyard match the photos that I gave you."

Parker simply let out a grunt.

"Okay, then . . . I was hoping you could answer

one other question for me." As we talked, I watched as Lee stepped out a side door at the feed and seed. He had his phone to his ear as he spoke to someone, his motions nearly frantic.

Interesting.

I glanced at Riley to see if he was seeing what I was.

He nodded.

"I'm not promising anything," Parker mumbled, bringing my thoughts back to this conversation.

I mentally ran through all the questions I needed answers to and picked the most pertinent one. "Can you tell me the name of the owner of the storage shed that I purchased at auction?"

"No."

That was fast. "Are you sure?"

"Positive."

"But—"

"Gabby, you don't need this information." His words were biting.

I frowned. "Maybe I need to contact this person."

"Why would you need to do that?"

My thoughts raced through possible excuses. "Because . . . maybe he or she wants these photos."

"The storage unit owner can get them to him or her."

"I'm going to find out this name one way or another," I reminded Parker. "You know that."

He let out a sigh. "Yes, I'm sure you will. That doesn't mean I need to make it easier for you."

"But you could make it easier, couldn't you?" I knew my argument probably wouldn't get me anywhere, but I tried anyway.

He sighed again, this time the sound came out longer and more drawn out. "Listen, don't make me regret this. Her name was Addie Patrick."

Something about the way he said the words caused my breath to catch. "Her name *was*? As in past tense?"

"Five months ago she died in a home invasion."

My heart pounded as I processed that thought. "I guess her family never came to claim her belongings . . ."

"She didn't tell anyone she had rented the space. Apparently, the storage unit sent three letters about payment, letting her know it would go up for auction. But either no one got those letters, or no one cared."

"Did she have any connection to Billy O'Brien?"

Parker remained quiet a moment before finally saying, "You're going to have to figure that one out yourself. Although if I were you, I'd leave this one to the police."

"Why is that?"

"It's an unsolved cold case," he told me. "The killer has gotten away with this crime for two years. I'm sure he doesn't want to be caught now—not when he's so close to getting away with this."

"Was Addie the killer?" I didn't really expect Parker to answer that.

"Good luck, Gabby."

Then he ended the call.

I'd asked if Addie was the killer. However, I didn't think that was the case.

I didn't have a lot to go on here. Just assumptions and gut feelings, which weren't reliable.

But based on the angle of that gunshot wound, the person who'd pulled the trigger had been taller than Billy, who was six foot two inches. Most women wouldn't be the right height.

I needed to let that thought simmer for a moment.

As I did, I relayed my conversation with Parker to Riley.

TWELVE

RILEY and I sat in silence for a few minutes, each lost in our own thoughts. Riley was researching something on his phone and kept saying, "Give me a minute."

I was totally giving him a moment.

But I couldn't wait to hear what was on his mind. I loved the way his brain worked.

"Get this," Riley murmured, still staring at his phone. "It turns out that Trudy O'Brien still lives in this area."

"Trudy O'Brien?" I thought I'd heard that name before, but I had too much on my mind right now to remember where.

"She owns the house where Billy O'Brien was shot."

Realization dawned on me. That was right! "Billy and Trudy are siblings . . ."

Riley nodded. "That's right. Stepsiblings, it appears. I haven't dived into their family history or anything. But maybe we could talk to her. Maybe she knows something or can give us some insight into Billy's death."

I *loved* that idea. "How far away does she live?"

"My phone says fifteen minutes away. I know there are no guarantees we'll catch her at home, but it can't hurt to try." He glanced up at me as if waiting for my reaction.

Those sounded like famous last words.

But that wasn't going to scare me off.

However, as we took off down the road, I glanced in my sideview mirror.

And that's when I saw a yellow Trans Am behind us.

My gut tightened.

It was the man from the auction.

He was following us.

I was sure of it.

———

"I see him," Riley muttered.

"Why is this guy following us?" Tension threaded

through my muscles.

"I have no idea. But I don't intend on letting him catch us."

"What are you going to do?"

He glanced to his side before suddenly turning off the interstate and heading toward downtown Norfolk. I had no idea what he was planning.

But sure enough, the Trans Am followed us.

This guy was crazy, wasn't he? That was the only explanation I could think of.

Riley turned on a one-way street between some high rises. He knew this area well.

I hoped that worked to our advantage.

But the Trans Am followed.

Great.

At least the driver wasn't being aggressive.

Not yet, anyway.

Riley turned again. Then again.

The Trans Am stayed a safe distance behind us.

But it was still there.

"I see a way to lose him," Riley muttered.

The next instant, he headed toward a Tide crossing—the Tide was Norfolk's commuter train.

As he did, the gates began coming down.

I closed my eyes.

Were we going to make it?

I wasn't sure.

WE MADE it through the train crossing.

We lost the Trans Am.

And we pulled onto the street where Trudy O'Brien lived.

My heart still raced with adrenaline from the danger. I was thankful Riley had expertly maneuvered the situation.

Trudy lived in an old farmhouse located on a relatively large parcel of land—I'd guess at least ten acres—positioned between the Elizabeth River and Interstate 264. Properties this large were nearly nonexistent in Norfolk. The land must have been grandfathered in, if I had to guess.

A "For Sale" sign stood in the front yard.

Riley and I climbed from his car and started

toward the porch. But before we reached the door, it opened.

A petite woman holding a shotgun stood there sneering at us.

She was probably twenty-five years old and slim, with blonde hair that framed her face in big curls.

Yet somehow the woman seemed much older than she probably was. Maybe it was the early lines on her face or the toughness in her eyes. Maybe grief had matured her faster than her peers.

I wasn't sure.

An aura of country smarts surrounded her. That was what I called homegrown people who were used to taking care of themselves. If I had to guess, this woman knew how to survive on the land, fix a car, and repair a dishwasher.

She also knew how to defend her property—and herself.

I hoped that didn't come back to bite us, I thought as I stared at her shotgun.

"What are you doing on my property?" she demanded, her eyes narrowed in an "I dare you" attitude.

Riley lifted his hands and pushed me slightly behind him.

"We don't mean any harm," Riley started. "But

we were hoping to ask you a few questions about your brother. Or should I say your stepbrother?"

She lowered her gun ever so slightly. "Billy?"

"We're trying to piece together what happened to him," Riley said.

"Who are you?"

"I'm Riley Thomas, a lawyer, and this is my colleague, Gabby St. Claire."

Trudy glanced at us skeptically, as if trying to ascertain whether or not she believed our explanation.

I waited for her reaction, hoping this didn't turn ugly.

———

After a few tense moments, Trudy finally lowered her shotgun and nodded at the porch. "Fine. I'll talk. But it's going to have to be out here. I don't let strangers into my house. Not after what happened to Billy."

That made me wonder if she believed there had been strangers involved in his death. But I didn't ask those questions. Not yet.

I could respect her decision to talk to us on the porch. In fact, I was simply happy that she was talking to us at all.

Riley and I sat on a bench swing while Trudy sat

in a ratty-looking wicker chair across from us. She set her gun on the cement patio beside her, almost as if she wanted to remind us that the weapon was there and that she could use it if necessary.

The thought wasn't especially comforting, but I told myself that Trudy was just paranoid. Anyone who'd had a family member murdered would be.

"What do you want to know?" Trudy's words sounded clipped and slightly uncultured.

She definitely had a gruffness about her that surprised me. For some reason, I'd pictured someone petite and quiet—probably because I'd known a Trudy in elementary school and that's what she'd been like.

Riley gave me a glance, letting me know that I could take the lead.

I cleared my throat, hoping I didn't blow this. "We've come across some new evidence, and as soon as I heard that this case hadn't been solved, I was immediately interested."

Trudy glanced at Riley. "Is she a PI or something? I heard law firms hire them sometimes."

He offered a stiff nod. "Something like that."

"What kind of new evidence did you find exactly?" A good dose of skepticism still stained her gaze.

"We found some pictures, although we're not

clear what the photos are of or why they're important," Riley said.

"Pictures?" A spark of interest lit her gaze. "Can I see them?"

"Of course." I pulled them from my purse and handed them to her.

I watched as Trudy flipped through them, trying to see if any of them seemed to trigger anything inside her.

I hoped this was the moment we might get some answers.

WHEN TRUDY WAS DONE, she shook her head and handed the photos back to me matter-of-factly.

"I'm sorry, but I didn't see anything of significance," she said. "A couple pictures that look like they were taken outside my other family house. But that doesn't really tell me anything about what happened there, however."

"We're still trying to figure out their importance," Riley said.

"We also found a map," I added. "Your old house was marked on it as well as a feed and seed store."

"Okay . . ." Trudy squinted as if she wasn't sure where I was going with this.

"And we discovered a gun that's now being tested to see if it's the murder weapon," I added, hoping I didn't regret sharing that update. It was too late now. The information was already out there.

Her eyes widened just a second before her entire body seemed to slump. "Is that right?"

She offered no other reaction. Was that because she didn't know what to think? Or because she was covering up her true feelings?

"Is there anything that you can tell us about the investigation that may not have been in the newspapers?" Riley shifted toward her, firmly planting his feet so the swing didn't glide anymore.

Trudy ran her hand through her hair and looked off in the distance, almost as if this news had shaken her. "I'm just so torn up still about Billy. He was my only relative. Sometimes, I still can't believe he's gone."

"Were the two of you close? He was your stepbrother, correct?" I continued to study her face.

Was she still grieving? Did she and Billy get along? They were stepsiblings, after all. Children who were part of blended families didn't always like each other. What had their relationship been like?

Trudy shrugged. "I don't know if I'd say we were close. I was nine, and Billy was eight when our parents got married. At first, we couldn't stand each other. Then we became closer after my dad died. I guess that kind of bonds you with someone, right?"

"Yes, it does," I told her.

I'd lost my own mother, so I knew about grief. However, my mom's death hadn't brought my dad and I closer. Mostly because he started drinking too much. He stopped a few times and vowed to do better, only to go back to his old ways.

I turned my attention back to the woman in front of me, trying to focus my thoughts.

"How old were you when your dad died?" I asked, trying to put together a timeline in my head.

"I was sixteen. Billy was fifteen. Dad had a heart attack." She pressed her lips in a straight line. "And then Billy's mom died in a car accident three years later."

"I'm sorry to hear that." Those were two huge losses.

"Thanks." She glanced at the floor as a forlorn expression filled her eyes.

"After high school, where did Billy live?" I asked, trying to carefully change the subject. "Not with you, right?"

"As a matter fact, he lived here." She glanced beside her at the house. "This was my father's property before he got remarried. My dad held onto it since the land had been in the family for a long time. Many, many people have tried to buy it, but my dad never wanted to sell. Anyway, Billy loved it out here. He wanted to have his own micro farm one day."

So that might explain the feed and seed. Maybe that store *was* a place Billy had frequented. But if that was the case, wouldn't Lee have recognized him?

I stored that question away in the back of my mind.

"We saw the For Sale sign," Riley said.

Trudy shrugged nonchalantly. "I tried to hold onto it for as long as I could. But there are just too many bad memories here."

"I understand," Riley said. "The house where Billy died . . . that belonged to you too?"

"It's all a little confusing, to be honest. It was actually Billy's house."

We must have looked confused because she laughed.

"That house was where Billy's mom, Evelyn, lived before she met my father and remarried."

"Where did you all live after Evelyn married your dad?"

"We lived at Evelyn's house—we called it the City House and this one the Country House. She didn't like this old house. Partly it was because my mom lived here before she left us when I was four. Evelyn couldn't handle the idea of living in my mom's shadow. I didn't understand it when I was little, but I guess it makes sense now."

"Right," I murmured.

"After high school, Billy asked me if he could live here at the Country House." She glanced at the farmhouse behind her. "I told him yes. I mean, this place was rundown at that point. No one had lived in the house for ten years—unless you count a few renters that basically destroyed the house. Dad would come here and garden, and Billy always came with him. Anyway, Billy said he wanted to fix it up."

"What was Billy doing at the City House the day he died?" I pulled my coat closer as a cool breeze swept across us.

"I'm not sure." Trudy frowned and stared into the distance as if the past had swept her back in time. "I was still living there, but I wasn't home from work yet. I'm a teacher—don't become one unless you like low-paying jobs with few advancement opportunities."

"I'm sure that can be tough," Riley muttered.

"It is." Trudy drew in a deep breath. "Anyway, Billy and I were going to meet for dinner that night at six. I had swung by the store to pick something up, but I got caught in traffic. By the time I got home . . . police cars were everywhere." She rubbed her throat as if it burned. "Billy was dead."

———

I gave Trudy as much time as she needed to compose herself. I could see she was struggling, and I couldn't blame her.

Grief was hard.

Finally, she glanced back up as if indicating we could continue.

"Do you know how long he'd been dead when you arrived?" I regretted the blunt question, but I needed to know.

"Based on what I remember, the police placed his time of death at about four o'clock. So he must have gone over to the City House and decided to wait in the backyard. He always said he felt more at peace when he was out in nature. Back then, I used to have this aqua green metal chair underneath that live oak. Billy liked to go there and think."

"Had there been anything bothering him in the weeks before his death?" Riley asked. "Any problems? From what I understand, he was a pretty laid-back guy that people seemed to really like."

"He was." She sniffed. "He couldn't have hurt a fly."

"The police named Bruce Clemmons as a suspect," I said. "They think he killed Billy in order to gain access to his finances."

She snorted. "I don't believe that. My brother didn't have any money. Why would anyone target him? I mean, if you want to rob someone, find someone who looks rich, at least."

She might have a point.

"Was there anyone you thought could have done this?" I tried to confirm.

That's when Trudy's gaze became stormy. "Cody West."

"Cody?" It was the first time I'd heard his name.

Her entire countenance shifted, and rage consumed her face. "Cody was Billy's best friend . . . and I believe he's the one who killed my brother."

MAYBE THIS WAS the information I was looking for. It was clear Trudy believed Cody was guilty. I was anxious to find out more.

"Why do you believe Cody killed your brother?" I reminded myself not to hold my breath as I waited for her answer. But I couldn't wait to hear what she had to say.

"Over a girl." She rolled her eyes, her shoulders relaxing slightly. "Isn't it always about a girl?"

"Who is this girl?"

"Her name was Addie."

I sucked in a breath. Addie?

She was the one who'd rented that storage unit.

I tried to keep my expression level and not give away anything.

"What happened?" Riley asked.

"Cody was dating Addie. But as soon as Addie met Billy, the two of them hit it off. Addie broke up with Cody, and she and Billy began dating."

"That must have been hard—especially if Cody and Billy were close friends," Riley said.

"It was. But Billy really thought she was the one. He didn't want it to harm his friendship with Cody, but he ultimately thought the sacrifice was worth it."

"How did Cody take that?" I asked.

"Not well, as you can imagine. They got into a fist fight over it. I thought it would be over after that."

"But it wasn't?" Riley asked.

"I looked into Cody myself. Everyone said he was working at the time of the murder. He was a car salesman at a used car lot. But he had a fifteen-minute break."

"And you think he could have made it there to the house and shot your brother and then gotten back to work?"

"I tested the drive myself. It would have been tight. All the traffic lights would have to be just right. But it's possible."

"Did the police ever look into him?"

She scowled again. "His daddy's a police officer. And I believe that's the only reason no one has ever looked into him as a suspect."

Well . . . that was interesting.

"Do you by chance know where he is now?" Riley asked. "I would like to talk to him."

"You can talk to him, but don't be fooled by his charm. He moved out to Virginia Beach. Look him up. You'll find his address online."

At least we had another lead to follow.

I glanced at my watch. It was only three o'clock.

A lot could be accomplished in one weekend.

Could I add solving a crime to that list?

Or was I being foolish? Some of Norfolk's finest investigators had been on this case for two years, and they hadn't found any definitive evidence. Who was I to think that I could?

Even though that was an excellent question, another part of me deep down believed that I *could* find answers. I was smart. Determined. People liked to talk to me.

I was going to give that theory a test.

———

Riley still hadn't backed out of helping me, and I wasn't complaining.

We were in his car and headed down the road to try and talk to Cody West.

"What do you think about what Trudy said?" I started.

He let out a deep breath. "I don't know. I'm more curious than ever about Addie."

"It didn't sound like Trudy knew Addie was dead."

"It didn't. I suppose the two of them probably didn't keep in touch. But why would Addie have those items in her storage unit?"

"Did she kill Billy?" I asked.

"But what about the trajectory of the bullet?"

I frowned as I stared out the window.

Until an idea hit me.

"Trudy said there was a chair under that tree where he was shot. What if Billy was sitting down when he was shot? That could explain the trajectory of the bullet."

Riley rocked his head back and forth. "That could be correct. I mean, the chair is gone now. Was it gone when the police arrived at the crime scene?"

I crossed my arms. "It's almost impossible to know without seeing the crime scene photos."

And this was exactly why I wanted to be an official investigator. I wanted access to these things.

I knew I would be good at my job—I just needed my degree first so I could get one.

"And why does Trudy still own the house where her brother was killed?" Riley continued. "She lives on the other property now. I'm surprised she hasn't sold it."

"That's a good question. Some people like to shut out any memories of their grief and others like to hold on. Maybe she likes to hold on."

"Maybe." Riley rubbed his chin. "I just find it interesting."

"I also can't help but wonder if Lee knows more than he shared. That phone call looked pretty animated."

"It did. But we can't jump to any conclusions. Maybe he got a call about a delayed shipment or from an employee who always calls in sick or something."

I frowned before nodding. "You're right. That's exactly what it could be. I just find all of this so interesting . . ."

Finally, we pulled up to a townhouse located not far from one of the area's many military bases. Maybe Cody would provide some answers.

THERE WASN'T much parking out front of Cody's place, so Riley pulled perpendicular behind the other cars in the driveway. As he climbed out, he muttered something to the neighbor next door that he wasn't staying long—just in case the guy got rowdy about it.

Then we rang the doorbell at Cody West's house.

We waited, but there was only a dog barking. No answer.

After several minutes, I turned to Riley and frowned, ready to admit defeat. "It was worth a shot."

"It was." He frowned as he knocked on the door another moment.

"Are you looking for Cody?" someone asked in a loud, almost harsh voice.

We glanced at Cody's neighbor as he sat in a foldup chair with a cigarette between his fingers and a cloud of smoke around his head. If I looked close enough, I thought the words "lung disease" might appear in the haze. Based on the ashtray on the cement patio beside him, he'd already smoked at least an entire pack of cigarettes.

"We are." Riley stepped toward him, jamming his hands into the pockets of his jeans. "You don't happen to know where he is, do you?"

"Don't know for sure." The man took another long drag. "But I'd guess he's down at Finnegan's."

"Finnegan's?" I repeated.

"It's a bar down the street. He likes to walk there, even though it's a couple of miles away. That's where he usually is on weekends."

We thanked him and climbed back into Riley's car.

"Are you up for taking a trip there?" I asked. "I know you probably had other plans, and I don't want to totally bulldoze your time."

"Are you kidding? I have to know what happened, at this point. If I stop now, it will be like turning off the latest TV series I'm binging on before the final episode."

"I totally get that."

"And all this is because you *had* to buy that storage unit."

I grinned. "I just had a feeling I was going to win."

"You were right. Now look where you are."

I wasn't sure if where I was right now was a good or bad thing.

I set that thought aside. Instead, I said, "Okay . . . maybe I can find some answers. Maybe Trudy can sleep a little better at night knowing what actually happened to her brother."

We took off down the road. As we turned out of the neighborhood and onto a main thoroughfare, I saw Riley glance in his rearview mirror. I knew something was wrong.

Again.

"Riley?" My voice wavered as I said his name.

His grip tightened on the steering wheel. "I think we're being watched. Or followed."

I swung my head as I glanced over my shoulder, fully expecting to see the yellow Trans Am behind us again.

Instead, a dark gray sedan was there.

This was just a coincidence, right? Riley was seeing something that wasn't there.

So why did worry still linger inside me?

———

Several minutes of silence followed—tense silence.

Finally, I asked, "Why do you think someone is following us?"

"The driver has mirrored our every turn for the past ten minutes." As he said that last statement, he made a sharp left turn, barely missing oncoming traffic.

I gripped the armrest beside me as my blood pressure skyrocketed. "Riley . . ."

"Sorry about that." He glanced in the rearview mirror again. "I had to see if I could lose them."

"And did you?" Instead of listening for his answer, I glanced over my shoulder again.

Riley watched along with me.

A few seconds later, the gray sedan appeared again.

My heart beat harder.

We were being followed. Now there was no question about it.

But who was behind the wheel? The windows were tinted, and I couldn't tell who was inside. It could be a man, a woman, or Bigfoot, for all I knew.

"What are we going to do now?" I glanced at Riley as if I expected him to have some type of skill in defensive driving.

He was a lawyer, however. I had to give him props for his skills earlier today when the Trans Am had tailed us.

"We've got to figure out a way to lose him," Riley muttered. "I don't know what this guy wants, but it can't be good."

His words made a lot of sense. This person didn't simply want to know where we were going.

This driver wanted to silence us.

Maybe we were digging a little too deeply into this mystery. Making people uncomfortable. Stirring up trouble from a crime that someone thought had been forgotten.

Which probably meant that we were on the right track.

Riley made another sharp left turn, this time into a residential area.

This move could either pay off big time or it could get us trapped.

He couldn't go but so fast in the neighborhood. It wasn't safe.

Riley seemed to be on the same wavelength. He took another right.

Two right turns later, and we headed out of the neighborhood and back onto the highway.

When I glanced behind us, the sedan appeared again.

I fought back a frown. It was on us like a hornet whose nest had been disturbed.

We hadn't lost him. In fact, the driver seemed more determined than ever to make us pay.

An engine revved behind us.

"Hold on, Gabby!" Riley's jaw tightened.

The next moment, he jerked his car off the road.

His sedan rumbled as we jumped the curb and hit a sidewalk.

I braced myself for whatever would happen next.

CHAPTER
SEVENTEEN

I WAITED, anticipating the crash. Bracing for pain.

Nothing came.

Not yet.

Riley threw on the brakes, and we lurched to a stop.

Surreal silence surrounded us in the aftermath.

Was this what death felt like? Panic followed by peace?

I wasn't sure.

As the scent of burning rubber surrounded me, I realized I was far from dead.

I plucked an eye open and saw that Riley had somehow successfully managed to avoid hitting anything. And his car was completely off the road and on the sidewalk.

Traffic behind us continued like nothing had happened.

Life went on, despite the fact I'd almost died.

I sucked in a deep breath as I tried to collect myself.

"Are you okay?" Riley asked.

I nodded, my limbs shaky. "I think so. You?"

"Yeah, I guess."

That had been close.

Too close.

The only good news I could get from this was the fact that I had gotten the license plate number. And I needed to turn that over to Parker.

———

Riley and I remained in his car a few minutes before he eased off the sidewalk and back onto the road.

I'd halfway expected the police to show up or for someone to pull over and check on us.

No one did—both a relief and an irritation.

I mean, I didn't want to answer any questions. But did no one truly care?

I shoved that thought aside. I'd look at this as a blessing instead.

But right now, I needed to call Parker.

I didn't want to.

I was really sick of talking with him at this point. Every time I did, "You're so Vain" by Carly Simon began playing in my head.

But I called him anyway. Mostly because he was my best chance of finding out who was in that car.

He sounded just as enthusiastic as I expected when he answered. And by that I meant not enthusiastic at all.

"What now?" he grumbled.

I put the phone on speaker so Riley could hear the whole conversation.

I explained what had just happened, and Parker muttered several things under his breath before telling us he'd run the plate. But he wasn't at his computer now, so it was going to be a few minutes—maybe even an hour.

"Any updates on the serial number you found on that gun?" I rushed before Parker got off the phone.

"As a matter of fact, yes."

"Who did it belong to?"

"I can't tell you that."

I felt as if I could crawl out of my skin, travel through time and space, and clobber him on the other side of the phone line. "Oh, come on . . . I'm the one who found the gun."

"You weren't even looking for it."

"Minor detail."

He let out a sigh. "It belonged to Billy. There. Are you happy?"

Happy? I wasn't sure I'd take it that far.

I thanked him and, without further ado, I got off the phone. No need to draw that conversation out.

"I'm so glad you broke up with that guy," Riley muttered.

I glanced at Riley and blinked with surprise at his words—and the scowl on his face.

"You are?" He'd never said that to me before.

"It Only Takes a Moment" from *Hello, Dolly* began playing in my head.

Because Riley filled every one of my dreams of falling in love. I needed to douse those dreams with gasoline and set them on fire, however.

"He's a real jerk. You deserve someone who's better."

Something about his words made my cheeks heat. I knew Riley wasn't talking about himself when he made that statement. But still, a girl could dream. And I was.

Douse with gasoline, Gabby. Douse, douse, douse!

I WAS NEARLY breathless by the time Riley and I finally pulled up to Finnegan's.

Even though it wasn't a long drive, nearly getting run off the road had definitely upped my heart rate.

If I had to guess—which I kind of did—the person driving that car was the same guy who'd been following me. I really needed to find out his identity.

Because it was one thing to follow me to see what I was doing. But it was another thing to try and run Riley and me off the road.

I glanced at the bar. The white, cube-shaped building didn't have windows—or anything else of note on the outside either. It reminded me of one of those Styrofoam coolers my family used to bring to the beach when I was younger.

But Finnegan's was written in a cursive font on the green neon sign over the double glass doors at the front.

This was the place.

Riley stared at it, a touch of hesitation in his gaze until he finally said, "Let's do this."

He glanced at me, and our gazes met.

Something flickered in his eyes—a moment of connection. Maybe even attraction?

Or was I only seeing what I wanted to see?

My cheeks heated, and I looked away.

Douse, douse, douse! That was going to be my new saying.

It wasn't that I didn't think I was good enough for Riley—I just didn't think I was his type. He needed someone who wasn't as damaged as I was.

But the truth was, I needed someone exactly like him.

And that was the irony of life sometimes.

I cleared my throat as I realized I'd probably made the whole moment awkward by gazing into his eyes for too long.

Besides, Riley had been keeping his distance lately. He was probably trying to make a point, to be careful around me so I didn't get my heart broken.

We stepped inside Finnegan's, and I immediately didn't like the place. It was dark, the music was too loud, and the people were too drunk. And it was only four o'clock in the afternoon. I could hardly imagine what it might be like at night.

I had a feeling sailors liked to grace this place. It was close enough to one of the local bases that it would be convenient for them.

Riley and I got a few weird glances that made me wonder if everyone else here knew each other.

The bartender yelled for us to take any seat we could find, and we headed toward a high-top table in the corner.

As we walked there, I searched the place, looking for Cody. I'd looked up his photo before we came. He should be a few years older now than the last picture I had seen, but I had a basic idea of how he looked.

In the photo, he had had a scruffy beard and mustache, and he had been wearing a sloppy T-shirt. He had a round face, pale skin, dirty-blond hair, and a touch of acne.

Riley and I sat down, and I continued to scan the room.

That's when I spotted him.

Cody West.

He sat at a pub-style table with two other guys, drinking and laughing a little too loudly.

Maybe our luck would finally turn.

———

Cody was here, and three bottles of beer littered the table in front of him. Based on how loud he talked and how his words slurred, he'd already downed all of them.

Maybe more.

That could make things either better or worse. Sometimes alcohol loosened people up and helped them to say things they might keep inside otherwise. Other times it made them mean.

I had a feeling Cody was one of the overly friendly ones, however.

Riley and I ordered some soft pretzel bites, nachos, and soda, to start with. I was getting hungry and might need to order more if we stayed here long enough. While we waited for our server to bring them, we made our way over to Cody.

His eyes widened as soon as he saw us before quickly narrowing with suspicion. "Who are you, and why are you trying to talk to me?"

Maybe my overly friendly theory was incorrect. So much for intuition.

"We're not here to cause trouble," I started, keeping my voice gentle. "I just wanted to ask you some questions."

"Is this about Billy's death? Because every once in

a while, I have a reporter or podcaster come around, and they want answers. I don't have anything to say. I don't know how much clearer I can make that."

"We're not reporters, podcasters, or even with the police department," Riley said. "But we'd like to talk to you anyway."

Cody eyed us as if trying to figure out if we could be trusted.

That's when I knew I had one last chance to plead my case.

"We're looking into Billy O'Brien's death, trying to figure out what really happened. We want to do what the police couldn't."

"You mean put me behind bars?" Cody's words came out at a growl.

"Not at all," I told him. "We're looking for the truth."

Everything I said was true. I had no opinions as to whether or not Cody was a suspect or if he had killed Billy.

I only wanted to ask questions.

"So who are you?" Cody asked.

"I'm a lawyer," Riley said.

Thank goodness he had that excuse to use. It sounded much better than mine: I'm a crime scene cleaner. That wouldn't get me nearly as far.

"You take *pro bono* cases?" Cody asked.

"Sometimes," Riley said.

Cody observed Riley another moment.

I held my breath as I waited for his response.

Maybe I should have left the closing argument to Riley.

VAN HALEN'S "Where Háve All the Good Times Gone?" played overhead as we waited for Cody's answer.

Finally, he told the guys around him, "I'll be back."

He followed Riley and me back to our table, where our pretzels, nachos, and sodas were already waiting. We all sat and, without invitation, Cody popped one of the pretzel bites into his mouth.

Then he turned and looked at both of us. "What do you want to know?"

"What do you think happened to your friend?" I cut right to the chase, knowing my time could be limited.

"I'm not sure. But I didn't do it. I would never kill

my friend. Never!" He sliced his hand through the air. "Billy and I were close like brothers."

"Until Addie came into the picture." Riley let his statement hang out there.

"It wasn't like that." He scowled, his face reddening with the expression.

"I heard it caused a rift between you and Billy, one that couldn't be mended." I picked up a pretzel and took a small bite—just in case I needed to jump in again.

He ran a hand through his hair. "I was mad. I'm not going to lie about that. Addie was my girl, you know? And friends don't do that. Bros before—"

"I get it," I told him, stopping him before he finished that despicable statement.

His eyes remained glazed and unfettered by the way I'd cut him off. "Anyway, I happened to see them together once. And you know what? They were good together. They both looked happy. I thought one day I might even be able to give them my blessing."

"But you were missing from work around the time of the murder. How do you explain that?"

His gaze darkened. "People say I could have gotten to the house and done it, but that would be crazy. I could barely drive there and back in that amount of time, not to mention the fact I would have needed time to confront Billy, kill him, clean myself up, *and* hide the murder weapon. Do I look like Houdini?"

He had a point.

"Why does Trudy seem so sure it was you?" Riley asked.

He shrugged tersely. "She's never liked me. Well, the truth is, she liked me *liked me* back when we were in high school. But she wasn't my type. She's had a chip on her shoulder ever since then."

Maybe that made sense. But that was an awfully big chip to go from being rejected by your crush to accusing him of murder.

I pulled up some pictures on my phone and showed them to Cody. "Ever seen this T-shirt before?"

He didn't have to look at it long. "I have. Mr. O'Brien took Billy and me on a fishing trip down in the OBX about two months before he died. We all got T-shirts like that—FCB stands for Frank's Charters on the Banks—so we could remember the trip. It was a great time."

Good to know. But I had more questions.

I showed him the picture of the bullet hole in the side of the house. "Any idea what this is?"

He didn't answer so quickly this time. "Not really. Billy was a hunter, and he loved guns. Anyone who was interested? He'd teach them to shoot. Sometimes there were mishaps, however. Maybe that was one of them."

"Any idea where that picture was taken?" Riley asked.

Billy shook his head. "No, sorry."

I shifted my thoughts. "Who do you think murdered your friend?"

His gaze darkened again. "I have theories, but the police never listened to me."

"I'm listening now."

He thrust his jaw forward as he seemed to contemplate his words. Finally, he said, "I always thought the police should look at Steve."

"Who's Steve?" Riley asked.

"Addie's older brother. I don't think he and Billy liked each other. He thought his sister could do better."

"Would that be worth killing over?"

Cody shrugged. "In the heat of the moment? Possibly."

———

"Okay," I started as I turned to Riley once we were back in his car. "I know you're probably getting tired of investigating with me, but I really want to talk to

Addie's friends or family or someone who knew her. Maybe somebody knows why she got that storage unit."

Riley didn't even hesitate before saying, "I'm in."

That was what I was hoping he would say.

"Great." My reaction sounded lame, but that was okay. I typed Addie's name into my phone and found an old address for her. "128 Blue Angel Drive. Should we go there?"

"Why not?"

This time as we rode down the street, I felt tenser than I had earlier. I kept waiting for that sedan to pop up. Maybe even the Trans Am.

But neither car appeared.

However, darkness was falling right now, and the upcoming evening skies would make it easier to conceal any vehicles, which didn't bring me any comfort.

Finally, Riley and I pulled up to a two-story home with vinyl siding, located in Virginia Beach near the Norfolk city line.

The house looked normal and well-kept with some evergreens in the flowerbed and a cheerful "Welcome" sign near the door.

I hoped talking to Addie's family wouldn't be a mistake. Normal house, normal family . . . right?

I was about to find out.

With Riley by my side, we climbed up the steps and rang the bell.

A woman in her late fifties answered, a pensive expression on her face. "Can I help you?"

I knew being here right now wasn't ideal. It was dark outside and going to some stranger's house unexpectedly at this hour was enough to make anybody cautious.

"I'm sorry to bother you," I started. "I know this could be a bad time, and I should've called first. But I was hoping to ask you some questions about your daughter."

"Addie?" Her expression went flat. "What do you want to know about Addie?"

I knew that her death was still raw, as it should be. She hadn't passed away that long ago.

"Were you friends of hers?" the woman asked.

I glanced at Riley, and I knew we just needed to tell the truth here.

"We're not," I told her. "But I bid on a storage unit, and it turns out it belonged to your daughter."

"She had a storage unit?" She blinked as if confused—which didn't surprise me since no one had claimed it.

"That's my understanding."

"I'm confused." Mrs. Patrick shook her head, her

short, lifeless hair swishing with the movement. "What was inside?"

"That's the strange thing. There wasn't very much inside. Just a camera, a map, and a shirt." I waited for her reaction, desperate to see if it would tell me anything.

"Camera? We got her a camera for her eighteenth birthday, but she hardly ever used it. The times she did . . . well, she didn't exactly have a knack for taking photos. Most of them were blurry or accidents."

That certainly fit what I'd seen with those documents and the random foot picture.

"I wondered where it went after she . . ." Mrs. Patrick rubbed her throat. "After Addie passed."

"The police have it right now, but I imagine they'd give it back to you."

"I'm still not sure exactly why you are here." She stared at me. "To ask me about the storage unit?"

I knew I needed to proceed very cautiously and sympathetically here.

But before I could ask any more questions, a car pulled up on the street in front of the house. I barely paid attention until I heard a door slam.

As I looked over, I saw that it was a . . . yellow Trans Am.

And the driver was storming right toward us.

RILEY GRABBED my arm as he saw the car and pushed me behind him.

I knew what he was thinking.

That we were in serious trouble.

Probably because we were.

Should we run? Had we just put Mrs. Patrick in danger also?

My thoughts raced.

"Steve, you're home early," Mrs. Patrick murmured, her voice softening.

I glanced at Mrs. Patrick, not bothering to hide my confusion. "Steve?"

She blinked. "My son."

Her son? This man was related to Addie?

Did he think we had something to do with his

sister's death? Had he been searching for just the right opportunity to make us pay?

My heart still pounded out of my chest. I had no idea what was going to happen right now. Would we be ambushed?

The man paused on the sidewalk and glowered at us. "What are *you two* doing here?"

"You all know each other?" His mom said as she rubbed her hands together nervously.

"He's been following us all day," I muttered.

"What? Steve?" Mrs. Patrick glanced at him.

His jaw tightened as his scowl deepened. "It's a long story."

"Steve . . ." his mom muttered.

His gaze met mine then Riley's. "How about if the three of us talk in private? There's no need to get my mom upset."

I wasn't sure if talking to this guy in private was a good idea or not. But I did think that trying to keep Mrs. Patrick calm was a fantastic idea.

"Why don't you go inside, Mom?" Steve glanced at her, sounding like a decent human as he said the words. Maybe he was a good faker. "I'll handle them."

Handle them? To me, that sounded like the same thing as "I'll kill them."

Mrs. Patrick glanced at him before nodding. "I'd love that camera back, if you don't mind."

"I'll let the detective know to give it to you when he's done with it. I promise."

She nodded before slipping inside and closing the door.

Then it was just Steve, Riley, and me.

Steve crossed his arms as he stared at us. "Why are you bothering my mom?"

"The better question is why have you been following us?" Riley asked. "Trying to run us off the road."

"What?" Surprise laced his voice. "I didn't do that."

"Sure, it wasn't in your yellow car," Riley continued. "But who else would try to kill us?"

"Why would I want to kill you?" He sounded earnestly confused.

"If you weren't trying to kill us, then what were you trying to do?" Riley also sounded earnestly confused.

And I felt confused, so we were all in the same sinking boat right now.

"I wanted to know what was in that storage unit that my sister got. I only found out about it the day before the auction. At that point, it was too late to back pay on it. Plus, I wanted to keep it on the downlow who I was. Just in case . . ." He shrugged. "You know."

I did know.

Just in case a killer might be watching.

"Why not just have a conversation?" Riley asked. "Why all the cloak-and-dagger stuff?"

"I looked you up. Saw you solved a crime. At first, I was suspicious of you. Then I realized you were probably investigating. I wanted to know what you found out."

Maybe I could buy that story.

Maybe.

I was reserving final judgment.

"There wasn't very much in the unit. Certainly not worth four hundred dollars." I crossed my arms this time. "Why don't you tell us what's going on?"

"I'm trying to figure out what happened that may have gotten my sister killed. That's what I'm doing." He shrugged stiffly, his gaze daring us to argue.

My heart beat harder. I thought this guy was telling the truth. I didn't think he actually wanted to hurt us.

Maybe I needed to hear him out.

———

"Do you have any theories?" I started.

Steve sat on the edge of the porch and let out a deep breath. "Addie was obsessed about Billy's murder. I knew she was upset, but now I'm beginning to wonder if she started investigating."

Realizations pummeled me.

Suddenly, it made sense. That evidence in the storage locker hadn't been left by a killer.

It had been left by Addie, who was investigating her boyfriend's murder. She must have stored everything she discovered in that unit in hopes it wouldn't be found or destroyed . . . by the killer.

Before she could take it to the police, she'd been murdered herself.

Riley and I exchanged a glance, and I knew the two of us were on the same page.

Riley turned back to Steve. "Did she tell you anything about her investigations?"

"Not really. One day, she came home, and she was muddy. I asked her what she'd been doing. She looked out of sorts—that's the best way to describe it. She said she remembered something Billy had told her once and decided to dive into his past. Said something about making his wishes come true."

"She didn't tell you what that entailed?" I asked.

He shook his head. "No, she didn't."

"Did Addie ever mention who she thought might have killed Billy?" Riley asked.

Steve shrugged as tight lines formed on his forehead. "She had asked me to meet that night at her favorite Greek restaurant. But when I went there, she never showed up. I went by her house, and I'm the one who . . . I, you know. I found her. Dead."

I swallowed hard. "I'm so sorry to hear that."

Steve's throat looked tight as he nodded. "Me too."

"Did the police ever have any suspects in your sister's murder case?" I asked.

He scowled. "They put a man named Larry Matthews behind bars. He was involved with several other robberies in the area, but he never admitted he killed Addie."

"Do you think her death was linked to Billy's?" Riley asked.

Steve shrugged. "I definitely think it's a possibility."

"Did you have any theories about what happened to Billy?" Riley asked.

"I don't know." Steve ran his hand through his hair. "I've given it a lot of thought, and I still don't know."

"Were you and Billy even friends?" I asked.

"Not really. I didn't like anyone that my sister dated." He straightened. "And when I say I didn't like him, that doesn't mean I would kill him. She was my little sister. No one was good enough for her. But Billy seemed like a decent guy. He worked hard, he loved cars—we had that in common—and he was pretty sentimental. He saved the straws from the first date he and Addie went on. Saved all her notes. He really seemed to like her."

"It sounds like you and your sister were close," I murmured. "Did you talk a lot?"

"We did. All the time." He choked on the words a moment. "Sometimes, I still can't believe she's gone."

I gave him a few seconds before asking my next question. "Did you ever notice anything strange about Billy or the way he was acting before he died?"

Steve hauled in a deep breath, some focus returning to his gaze. "I've been thinking about that a lot since she passed. I really thought the police's theory that he just happened to be in the wrong place at the wrong time was accurate for the longest time. But now I believe that Addie found out something the police couldn't."

"Any idea what?" Riley asked.

"I know the day before Billy died, he had an argument with someone."

"Are you talking about his friend Cody?"

"No, it wasn't Cody. It was someone from the feed and seed store."

My eyes widened, but I tried not to show my surprise. "Do you know who?"

"I'm not sure. But Billy was hot about something. And I know what your next question will be. What was the fight about? The truth is, I have no idea. He didn't say. Or if he did, Addie didn't tell me."

"Did he tell you anything else about it?" I nearly held my breath as I waited for his answer.

I felt like we were so close to finding at least some kind of lead. But if Steve didn't have any more information, then I was certain this could fizzle very quickly.

"All I remember him saying the last time we talked was that he wished his dad was still around so he could ask him some advice. Mr. O'Brien was like a real father to Billy. Billy even took his last name— that's how much he liked him."

I let that fact settle in my mind.

I could tell by the wariness on Steve's face that he didn't want to talk anymore. That grief was kicking in.

Riley and I told him we'd let him know if we discovered anything.

Steve thanked us, apologized for scaring us, and then we left.

The intrigue around the case was growing by the moment.

Riley and I sat in his car a moment after we said goodbye to Steve.

After taking several deep breaths, I turned toward him. "What do you think about that conversation?"

He sighed and ran a hand through his hair. "I think there's something Lee at the feed and seed store wasn't telling us. Was he the one Billy was arguing with?"

"Good question. And I'm inclined to agree with your thought. That location was marked on the map for a reason."

"Of course, Billy never said Lee's name. He just said someone at the feed and seed."

"We need to talk to him and find out what Lee says now."

Riley glanced at his watch. "It's already past six. Didn't you say it closed at that time?"

I frowned as I remembered checking the store's hours earlier. "Yes, you're correct. I guess we won't be talking to him today."

"How about tomorrow?"

My eyes lit with surprise. I hadn't expected Riley to say that. "I'd love to go talk to him tomorrow, but I know you're working. And I actually have a crime scene cleaning job lined up in the morning as well."

I was going to have to clean a whole bunch of crime scenes to pay back what I'd spent at that auction. Lesson learned.

"As soon as you're finished with that job, I'll take a lunch break and we can go together."

"You would do that?" That seriously made me crush on Riley even more.

"Oh, yeah. I'm fully invested now." He flashed a smile. "Like I said, we're on the last episode, and I've got to know what happens."

"I appreciate it."

His gaze caught mine. "Just promise me you won't go there alone."

I heard the grimness in his words and nodded. "I won't."

"Someone knows that you're getting closer to answers, and they don't like it. What I don't want to find out is how far they're willing to go."

"Believe me, I don't either." A shiver raced through me at the thought.

CHAPTER
TWENTY-ONE

CHAD DAVIS WAS my business partner. Today, the two of us were cleaning up a house where a domestic dispute had taken place. *Dispute* may have been putting it lightly, however.

A woman had shot her husband after he came at her with a knife.

The scene in the master bedroom was messy, to say the least. Chad and I would need to scrub the blood from the walls, tear up some carpet, and replace some drywall.

Chad had been a mortician in his prior life. He hadn't enjoyed the daily grind, so he'd moved here from West Virginia to start his own crime scene cleaning business.

We'd been direct competitors at first but had realized that we could be stronger together. So we'd joined forces.

So far, it was working out well.

While the soundtrack to *Little Shop of Horrors* played on my phone in the background, I told Chad about everything that had happened this weekend. He listened carefully.

He'd witnessed my shenanigans firsthand before.

"Is it just me or do mysteries seem to find you?" Chad paused with his razor in hand as he cut out a piece of carpet.

"Mysteries definitely seem to find me." I continued to scrub some blood off a wall while wearing my totally unflattering but entirely necessary hazmat suit.

"Any insights?" I asked. "You have experience with things like this. As a former mortician, is there anything strange about the angle of the bullet?"

He grunted as he pulled up a patch of carpet. "Not really. Not without seeing photos or an autopsy report."

His words made sense. "I'm unsure where to look right now."

"You know what they say. Follow the money."

"This Billy guy had no money." I paused from my scrubbing to catch Chad's expression.

It remained unchanged. He took death in stride

just about as easily as I did. When you worked with it day in and day out, it had a different effect on you. And it had to be that way. Otherwise, I'd come home every day with the weight of the world on my shoulders.

"What did someone have to gain by killing him?" Chad rocked back on his heels and looked at me, the carpet forgotten for a moment.

"Nothing. This Billy guy had no assets—no house, a junky car, a career that didn't pay much, and a stolen credit card."

Chad let out a hmm. "It's all very interesting. I'd say keep digging. I imagine you'll find something eventually."

I frowned. He was probably right. But how much time did I want to spend on this? I wasn't getting paid or anything. This was really just . . . fun. I mean, I'd be better off trying to pick up some extra jobs so I could raise money to make up for the four hundred I'd blown on the storage unit.

But this wasn't about money.

It was about principle. About finding answers. About the bad guys getting justice.

For that reason, I'd keep digging.

My thoughts were racing, and suddenly I couldn't wait to finish this cleanup.

―――――

Chad and I weren't finished hauling all our equipment back to my work van yet when he told me to go. He insisted that he could handle the rest of the job himself.

He clearly knew that I was anxious to find answers. I was that obvious.

He let me use his car, and I drove back to my apartment. I called Riley as I did, and he told me he'd meet me at the apartment in twenty minutes.

That was going to give me approximately ten minutes by the time I got back home to quickly shower and put on some clean clothes. I wouldn't have time to wash my hair, but that was okay. It had been back in a hood, and the crime scene hadn't smelled bad enough for my skin to absorb anything.

I slipped on my flip-flops just as I saw Riley pull up. I hurried downstairs to meet him.

Riley must have been able to tell I was excited when I climbed in the car because the first thing he asked was, "What did I miss?"

I shared Chad's theory with him.

"Interesting . . ." Riley mumbled.

Code for: he's given me something to think about.

We talked about our days as we drove to the feed and seed.

Today, it was significantly busier inside. But I spotted Lee in his overalls right away.

And he spotted us.

His gaze quickly darkened, and he looked away, almost as if he wanted to pretend we weren't there.

But Riley and I patiently waited in line for our turn so we could ask him some questions. Too bad it wasn't about mealworms or urban gardening.

However, there was a display of hammers right beside us. I had to keep that in mind, just in case . . . you know . . . things turned ugly.

Lee could grab one.

But so could Riley and I.

I hoped it didn't come down to that, however.

Finally, the other customers walked away. As soon as Lee turned to us, the friendliness left his eyes. "What do you two want?"

I braced myself for this conversation, having no idea where it would go.

I SUCKED in a deep breath before starting. "We were talking to an old friend of Billy O'Brien's, and he mentioned that you and Billy did know each other."

I studied Lee's expression, desperate to know if he'd try to lie to us again. But all I saw was a kind, grandfatherly figure.

"Your point?" Lee let out a sigh. "I'm pretty busy. This isn't really the best time for this conversation."

"My point is that you lied to us," I said. "Why do that? Unless you're hiding something."

"I didn't kill him, if that's what you're implying." His words didn't sound bitter. Maybe sad instead.

"To reiterate Gabby's question—then why lie?" Riley asked.

Lee let out a long breath, suddenly appearing exhausted. "The truth is, I *did* know Billy. He worked here for a while. But my wife is ill. Alzheimer's. Life has been tough these past several months, and I don't want to make it any tougher."

"I'm sorry to hear about your wife," I started. "When you told us you'd call us if she remembered anything, were you just trying to get rid of us?"

He nodded. "Yes, I was."

Part of me couldn't blame him. But I still had more questions. "Doesn't lying about Billy complicate things even more? Make them even tougher?"

"I don't want to get in the middle of the whole Billy drama. Of course, I want his killer brought to justice. But I'm losing hope it will happen in my lifetime. I already told the police anything I knew, which wasn't much."

"What was Billy like?" I decided to take a different tactic.

Lee let out another long breath and looked as if his mind were traveling back in time. "He was a nice kid. He loved farming. He struggled with his stepdad's death. His mom wasn't the same afterward."

I could relate to that.

"Last time Billy was here, it was three months before he died," Lee continued. "He wanted to know if I could recommend a lawyer."

I blanched. "What? Why?"

Lee puckered his lips in a frown. "I wish I could tell you. But I don't have any earthly idea."

I started to step away, but I stopped myself. "One more question. Who were you talking to on the phone after we left yesterday? The conversation looked tense."

I halfway expected his gaze to fill with anger. Instead, it filled with tears. "It was my wife's nurse. She was having a bad day, and I had to talk to her about some hard subjects. It had nothing to do with Billy."

I nodded. I believed him.

And if I was a praying woman, I would add him to my prayer list.

———

Just as we got back out to Riley's car, a familiar vehicle pulled into the lot.

This time, it wasn't a yellow Trans Am.

No, it was a red Viper instead.

Parker stepped out.

He scowled as soon as he saw me.

"Well, well, well." He paused in front of me. "If it isn't Nancy Drew and her little sidekick."

Riley returned Parker's scowl but was wise

enough not to respond. Any response would only feed Parker's insatiable need to put others down in order to raise himself up. Only the truly small did that.

"How's it going, Parker?" A chilly breeze washed over me as I said his name.

Good timing, God.

"I see you and I must be following some of the same leads." His jaw visibly tightened as he said the words.

"Glad to know you're on the right track."

He squinted. "Don't you mean that *you're* on the right track, not me?"

"No, I have no doubt about my abilities." I flashed a grin, knowing I was getting under his skin —which was exactly what I was going for.

His gaze darkened again. "You just think you're so clever, don't you?"

"I never said that."

"You didn't have to." He glanced at the store. "I already know you talked to Addie's family."

"I did. It looks like the contents of the storage unit were valuable after all—not in a financial sense. But valuable to this case. Speaking of which, Addie's mom would like that camera back when the case is closed."

"Noted."

"I told her it probably wouldn't be a problem."

Parker only grunted. "I'm really not sure why you're still investigating."

"Because I'm invested."

"If you get in my way, you know I'm going to have to arrest you."

I scowled this time. "Rude."

"Anyway, I've got to go talk to . . ." He probably started to say Lee but stopped himself. "*Someone* now. Anything I need to know?"

"Tell me what you know so far, and I'll tell you if you're missing anything . . ." I cocked an eyebrow as I waited for his response.

He practically growled. "Gabby . . ."

I shrugged. "What? It was worth a try."

"So?" Parker actually tapped his foot, acting like an impatient toddler.

I mean, I knew I was pushing his buttons, but really?

"Did Billy have anything valuable?" I asked. "Could money be the motivation?"

"I'm supposed to be the one asking questions."

I stepped closer, wishing he wouldn't brush me off. I needed answers. "Did he? I don't have access to his financials like you do."

His cold gaze met mine. "What do you think?"

"I can't see how he would. But then I thought

about his stepdad's death. I wondered if he received a payout from that." I mean, it could make sense, right?

"Now you're thinking like a detective." He turned. "I gotta go. Good luck—or not."

CHAPTER
TWENTY-THREE

I TURNED to Riley after Parker left. Neither of us had to say anything about Parker's behavior.

We both knew what the other was thinking: Parker was a total jerk.

But he seemed to have confirmed to us that we should follow the money as Chad suggested.

However, how were we going to find out where exactly that money was?

I wasn't sure.

"What now?" Riley asked.

"Don't you have to return to work?"

He glanced at his watch. "I still have another forty-five minutes. I mean, I'm officially my own boss now. But that doesn't mean I don't have work to do."

"I get that." I frowned as my thoughts raced.

"How do we find out if this crime was motivated by money . . . ?"

"I say we go talk to Trudy again. Maybe she can tell us something."

"Excellent idea."

We climbed into Riley's car and started down the road to her house.

She said she was a teacher, so there was a good chance she wouldn't be home right now.

We could try anyway.

As we turned onto the property several minutes later, Riley parked in the gravel driveway. We stepped outside and paused.

No cars were parked in front of the house, which seemed to indicate no one was home. Go figure.

Instead, I stared at the "For Sale" sign in the driveway.

"I wonder how Billy would feel about selling this property?" I murmured. "It sounds like this place was important to him, even though he hadn't grown up here."

"Trudy made it sound as if he loved it here."

Just then, a mint-colored BMW sped into the driveway before jerking to an abrupt halt. A woman dressed in a classy gray business suit stepped out.

She flashed a perfect smile at us as she slapped a "serious inquiries only" sticker on the For Sale sign.

"Oh, hello." She turned as if only then noticing we were staring at her.

I wasn't really sure how she'd missed us unless her oversized sunglasses were so dark, they blocked out everything.

"Are you interested in the property?" She smiled as if hopeful she might make a sale.

I glanced at Riley as I smelled an opportunity to get information. "As a matter of fact, yes, we are."

"That's wonderful. We've gotten so much interest in this place since it went up for sale. I knew we would. I've been telling Trudy for years that she's sitting on a fortune here."

I made a mental note to check how much this property was going for. "Is that right?"

"I mean, this is prime real estate. Right off the interstate? Check. Waterfront? Check. I told her we should get this zoned commercial, and she agreed. It's just a shame it took so long. There's *so much* red tape to jump through for those things."

"It sounds like rezoning was a great idea." Riley glanced back at the house.

Her smile faded, maybe because she realized she wasn't doing much to sell the property with all her talk about profiting off this sale. "What company are you with again?"

I was certain I didn't look as if I was with a very

prosperous company. Not in my T-shirt, cardigan, and jeans. Then again, maybe she truly couldn't see much through those glasses.

Either way, I needed to sound like I owned one of those startups that let employees come to work in bare feet, take naps whenever they wanted, and take unlimited vacation time.

"I'm with Alter, a startup tech firm that specializes in reaching teens through social media and engaging in mind control tactics in an effort to shape the belief of future generations," I finally said.

That sounded viable, right?

She stared at me a moment as if wondering if I was serious. Then she nodded with approval, almost appearing as if she liked that idea. "Sounds so interesting."

"Isn't it? Get them while they're young. That's our motto."

"Well, here's my card if you have any questions." She pulled something from the pocket of her blazer and handed it to me. "Right now, I've got to run."

As soon as she left, I turned to Riley.

Suddenly, I had a theory.

"What are you thinking?" Riley asked.

My thoughts suddenly felt laser focused. "I need to walk around the back of the house. And I want to look up this property, see how much it's worth."

Riley frowned before nodding. "Okay. Why not?"

That was the spirit. Why ask why when you could ask why not instead?

That was going to be my new motto.

"I'll look up the listing for this property in the meantime."

As he did that, I headed toward the back of the property.

I paused as my thoughts ran ahead of me.

Though the front of the house had a white vinyl exterior, the back had wood shingles, an addition that made it appear as if the place had been patched together haphazardly over the years.

I'd seen those shingles before.

In one of Addie's photos.

I stepped closer.

Was that a bullet hole in one of them?

My heart skipped a beat.

I was nearly certain it was.

"Get this," Riley muttered as he stared at his phone. "This property is going for three million dollars."

My eyes widened. That was even more than I expected.

"Three million is reason enough for murder." I nodded at the house. "And that's the bullet hole Addie took a photo of."

He followed my gaze. "Why would she take a picture of a bullet hole here, though? It's not as if the body was moved from the other house."

"I'm not sure. But she obviously thought she was onto something. Those other photos—the ones of the blurry documents? I wonder if they were photos of Mr. O'Brien's will? Or maybe even the deed to this property."

Riley didn't deny it. "Chad was right—follow the money. Do you really think Trudy would kill her stepbrother?"

My thoughts continue to race as I tried to connect the dots. "Billy *loved* this land. He wouldn't want to sell. But Trudy knew how much money she could make on it, and that's exactly what she wanted to do. She didn't make much as a teacher, so selling this property was her way out."

"But Trudy's dad owned this land. Do you think Mr. O'Brien left it to Billy instead of Trudy?"

"That's my best guess." Though I would need to think that one through a little more. "If Billy owned the land, Trudy had no rights to it. However, if Billy died . . ."

"There's a good chance the property would go to her," Riley finished.

"Then she could sell it and get the money she thought she deserved. However, since Billy died, there's been a lot of red tape to cut through in order to get it rezoned. Selling it for commercial purposes is really where she'll get the most bang for her buck."

We shared a glance.

That was when we heard a stick crack around the corner.

Before we could react, Trudy stepped into view.

She held a shovel like a baseball bat, and her eyes were full of hatred as she stared at us. "You should have never come here."

I STARED at Trudy as I tried to formulate what to do next.

Based on the look in her eyes, she wasn't in her right mind.

Had her desire for money gotten the best of her? Had guilt over killing her stepbrother taken a toll on her psyche?

"I was just throwing out theories," I finally said, hoping I could buy some time.

I knew Riley's phone was still in his hand, so I moved in front of him. Not so much because I wanted to protect him but because I hoped he might dial 911 without her seeing.

"I don't know what you're talking about." Trudy still held that shovel up as she glared. "All I know is that you are trespassing on my property, and that gives me the right to defend myself."

"I'm just trying to find out answers about your brother's death." I raised my hands. "You can't fault me for that, can you?"

"Sometimes it's best just to let these things go," she snarled. "This is one can of worms you should have never opened."

Okay, I wasn't going to convince her that I was simply snooping. She'd clearly heard me talk about my theory.

I needed to try a different tactic, one that I hoped might keep us alive.

"I'm guessing that your father saw just how much Billy loved this land," I said. "So he left it to your stepbrother, which completely offended you because he was *your* father."

Trudy's gaze darkened, but she said nothing.

"Then that real estate agent approached Billy and let him know exactly how much he could get from this property," I continued. "Billy did not like that idea. He didn't go along with it at all. But it would be the answer to all your problems. It's like you said, being a teacher doesn't pay very well. But you wouldn't have to work if you didn't want to if you sold this property. That's why you held on to the other house too, even after Billy's death. It went to you. You knew that you could move there one day if you sold this place."

Trudy's eyes narrowed, and she stepped closer, still holding that shovel. "How could you pass up three million dollars for this property? It was a no-brainer as far as I was concerned."

I looked around. I needed a way to get out of this situation.

As I remembered one of the pictures that Addie had taken, an idea hit me.

But it would take some careful maneuvering if my plan were to work.

I took another step back, easing Riley toward the path that I wanted him to go.

"So you told Billy to meet you there, and you arranged to pick up dinner, so you'd have a receipt to use as an alibi if things turned south. The timeline was tight, but you made it work. When you got here, you found Billy in the backyard waiting for you so you could talk. But he didn't see things your way, and the two of you got into an argument."

When Trudy didn't say anything, I continued.

"The angle of the bullet made it seem as if someone taller had shot him. In truth, he was sitting in the chair having some alone time when you confronted him."

Trudy's scowl deepened.

"You worried the conversation might turn ugly, so you'd grabbed Billy's gun before you left. Maybe you didn't even intend on using it. But you resented just how close your dad had been with Billy, didn't you? In the heat of the argument, you pulled the trigger. Then you realized exactly what you'd done, and you panicked."

"You think you have it all figured out, don't you?" Trudy scowled.

Actually, I did.

"For some reason, you were wearing Billy's T-shirt on the day of the murder. You quickly changed out of it after you shot Billy, and you stored the shirt in the cubby hole near the front door—the one under the milk stool. The police had no idea it was there, so they didn't even know to look."

Trudy let go of the shovel with one hand and wiped the moisture beneath her eyes. "Billy was a good stepbrother. I only wish the two of us could have seen eye to eye on things. It didn't have to be this way."

There you had it. A confession.

"Then Addie started looking into things, and you knew you were in trouble again," I continued. "You had to do something because she was getting too close to the truth—just like Riley and I are right now.

That's why you staged that home invasion. You were desperate for the money this land could bring you."

"I was fired after I lost my temper with my students one too many times. The school let me go. I haven't even begun to pay off my student loans, and I don't know what kind of job I'll be able to get. And why should I get another job? I'm sitting on a gold mine right here!"

"That sounds tough," I told her, even though I didn't quite mean the words.

"Enough talking!" Trudy's face reddened again. "I didn't come this far only to have my plan ruined by two strangers!"

With those words, she swung the shovel at us.

CHAPTER
TWENTY-FIVE

I DUCKED and the shovel missed my head by mere inches.

But I was going to have to put my plan into action a bit sooner than I'd anticipated.

I grabbed Riley's arm and moved him back, still trying to block the view of exactly where we were walking.

Trudy seemed so caught up in the moment that I doubted she would notice anyway. She was blinded by emotions and rage right now.

I needed to make that work in our favor.

"Gabby . . ." Riley muttered behind me.

"I got this," I whispered.

Based on the grunt he let out, he clearly didn't think I had this.

Trudy lunged at us again. "You're not going to ruin my plan!"

She swung, and we ducked.

But I heard the shovel slice through the air.

I could practically feel the pain that pointed metal tip would cause if it collided with my skin, my body.

I couldn't let that happen.

Riley and I could run.

That was tempting.

If my original plan didn't work, then that was what we would do.

But only a few more steps and . . .

I decided to take the leap. "Let's face the facts, Trudy. Your love for money blinded you to anything else. Blinded you so much that money became the most important thing to you—more important than your brother even. That's why you killed him . . . so you could get your way. So you could sell this land and become a millionaire. I hope you can live with yourself knowing that."

Her cheeks reddened as more rage filled her gaze. "You don't understand!"

She let out a guttural yell.

Then she swung the shovel at us one more time.

As she did, I pushed Riley to the ground.

The momentum of her swing rocked her forward, and she lurched toward us to keep her balance.

As she did, her foot hit the edge of the old well.

The one you could barely see if it weren't for a small brick right beside it.

The one from the photos.

The one with the caution tape that had blown away, leaving it virtually unmarked.

Trudy screamed and the shovel flew from her hands.

She tumbled forward . . . and right into the hole in the ground.

She hit the bottom with a splash and several curses.

I heaved in a deep breath as adrenaline pumped through me.

Then Riley and I leaned over the well to check out the damage.

Trudy had only fallen about ten feet.

But it was far enough she wouldn't be able to climb out on her own.

She glared up at us, a mix of anger, fear, and desperation in her eyes.

"You've got to understand—I never meant for any of this to happen!" she shouted. "I only wanted the land that rightfully belonged to me."

Just as she said those words, sirens sounded in the distance.

It appeared Riley had been able to call 911 after all.

Now maybe this cold case could finally be closed, and those left behind in the wake of Billy's and Addie's deaths could find some peace.

———

"I had *no* idea where you were going with that," Riley muttered as the police took over the scene several minutes later. "I had to keep reminding myself that I could trust you."

I was so glad he'd done just that.

"I remembered seeing that well in the pictures Addie took," I explained as I watched the police pull a muddy Trudy from the ground amidst her cursing. "It didn't make sense until I saw it with my own eyes. But Steve mentioned something about Billy making a wish. That's when I knew that well was important. In fact, I have a feeling Trudy threw the gun into it after she shot Billy. It was a great hiding place—the police didn't find it two years earlier."

"It's certainly possible. Why didn't she hide the shirt and gun together?"

I thought about it a moment and shrugged. "Maybe she just wanted to make things more complicated. The more space she could put between the two pieces of evidence, the better."

"You could be right."

"I knew if we could just get Trudy close to it that we could trap her there," I explained. "I mean, sure, we could run. But that would mean Trudy could run too, and she might never be caught."

"That was some pretty quick thinking you did back there." His hand clamped on my bicep in an *attaboy!* type of way. "Good job, Gabby."

My cheeks heated at Riley's affirmation.

I was pretty good at this solving crimes thing. But it was more than that. When I investigated, I felt as if I'd found my purpose. I felt like it was what I was created to do.

Thankfully, I was working on my degree. Maybe one day I wouldn't have to be a crime scene cleaner. Maybe I could help people find closure from the worst moments in their lives through justice.

"The truth was right in front of us . . . half-truths, at least," I continued. "Addie must have started investigating and put the facts together. That ultimately led to her demise. It's just a shame that everything had to lead to this."

"I couldn't agree more. Give me an old apartment, student loan debt, and a job I love that doesn't pay great. I'll take that to the alternative."

That meant a lot coming from Riley, who'd at one time had a lucrative job and every nice thing he wanted. He'd admitted to me once that those things hadn't made him happy.

Parker strode up to us. Even with everything that happened, he still didn't look happy with me.

But I didn't care.

"I guess I should tell you, 'good job,'" he muttered as if the words were painful for him to say. His gaze darkened. "I would have figured this out. I just needed a little more time."

"Of course." I said the words to appease him. Because it didn't matter what I said, Parker believed his statement. And maybe he was right about eventually solving this crime. But maybe he wasn't.

As Parker walked away, I turned to Riley one more time. "You know what they say, don't you?"

"What's that?"

"Now it's Trudy's turn to cry."

He squinted. "Huh?"

"You know the old song, 'It's Judy's Turn to Cry?' It was written after 'It's My Party and I'll Cry if I Want To.'"

Riley stared at me, a blank look on his face.

I started singing, hoping he'd recognize the tune. He didn't.

But that was okay. I could educate him on '60s Billboard Top 100 songs later.

He glanced at his watch. "Well, I originally had forty-five minutes before I had to get back to work. Looks like I'm going to be about an hour late. Good thing my boss is pretty lenient."

"I don't know. I heard he was a stickler."

Riley grinned, and our gazes caught.

I forced myself to look away.

Douse, douse, douse, I reminded myself. Single, single, single!

"Anyway . . ." I cleared my throat. "That is good news. But you'd better get going. I don't want to keep you from doing what you love to do."

"Have I ever told you that life is always an adventure when you're around?" He raised his eyebrows as he turned to observe me, a lopsided grin on his face.

"I don't think you have . . ."

"Well, it is. And that's the whole truth."

~~~

Thank you for reading *Half Truth*. If you enjoyed this book, please consider leaving a review.
~~~

Stay tuned for *Half Empty,* coming next!

ALSO BY CHRISTY BARRITT:

YOU MIGHT ALSO ENJOY

...

THE SQUEAKY CLEAN MYSTERY
SERIES

On her way to completing a degree in forensic science, Gabby St. Claire drops out of school and starts her own crime-scene cleaning business. When a routine cleaning job uncovers a murder weapon the police overlooked, she realizes that the wrong person is in jail. She also realizes that crime scene cleaning might be the perfect career for utilizing her investigative skills.

#1 Hazardous Duty

#2 Suspicious Minds

#2.5 It Came Upon a Midnight Crime (novella)

#3 Organized Grime

#4 Dirty Deeds

#5 The Scum of All Fears

#6 To Love, Honor and Perish

USA Today has called Christy Barritt's books "scary, funny, passionate, and quirky."

Christy writes both mystery and romantic suspense novels that are clean with underlying messages of faith. Her books have sold more than four million copies and have won the Daphne du Maurier Award for Excellence in Suspense and Mystery, have been twice nominated for the Romantic Times Reviewers' Choice Award, and have finaled for both a Carol Award and Foreword Magazine's Book of the Year.

She is married to her Prince Charming, a man who thinks she's hilarious—but only when she's not trying to be. Christy is a self-proclaimed klutz, an avid music lover who's known for spontaneously bursting into song, and a road trip aficionado.

When she's not working or spending time with her family, she enjoys singing, playing the guitar, and exploring small, unsuspecting towns where people have no idea how accident-prone she is.

Find Christy online at:
www.christybarritt.com
www.facebook.com/christybarritt
www.twitter.com/cbarritt

Sign up for Christy's newsletter to get information on all of her latest releases here: **www.christybarritt.com/newsletter-sign-up/**

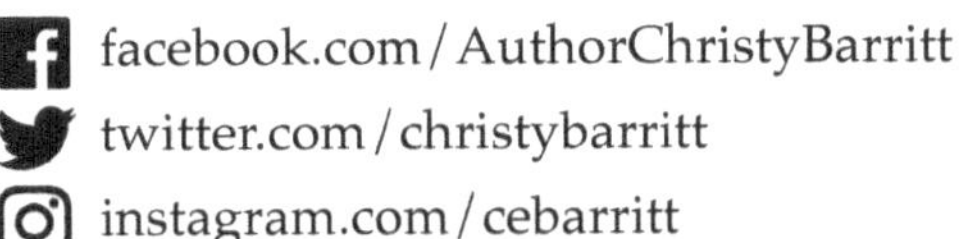

facebook.com / AuthorChristyBarritt
twitter.com / christybarritt
instagram.com / cebarritt

COMPLETE BOOK LIST

Squeaky Clean Mysteries:

    #1 Hazardous Duty

    Half Witted (Squeaky Clean In Between Mysteries Book 1, novella)

    #2 Suspicious Minds

    #2.5 It Came Upon a Midnight Crime (novella)

    #3 Organized Grime

    #4 Dirty Deeds

    #5 The Scum of All Fears

    #6 To Love, Honor and Perish

    #7 Mucky Streak

    #8 Foul Play

    #9 Broom & Gloom

    #10 Dust and Obey

    #11 Thrill Squeaker

    #11.5 Swept Away (novella)

#12 Cunning Attractions

#13 Cold Case: Clean Getaway

#14 Cold Case: Clean Sweep

#15 Cold Case: Clean Break

#16 Cleans to an End

While You Were Sweeping, A Riley Thomas Spinoff

The Sierra Files:

#1 Pounced

#2 Hunted

#3 Pranced

#4 Rattled

The Gabby St. Claire Diaries (a Tween Mystery series):

#1 The Curtain Call Caper

#2 The Disappearing Dog Dilemma

#3 The Bungled Bike Burglaries

The Worst Detective Ever

#1 Ready to Fumble

#2 Reign of Error

#3 Safety in Blunders

#4 Join the Flub

#5 Blooper Freak

#6 Flaw Abiding Citizen

#7 Gaffe Out Loud

#8 Joke and Dagger

#9 Wreck the Halls

#10 Glitch and Famous

#11 Not on My Botch

Raven Remington

Relentless

Holly Anna Paladin Mysteries:

#1 Random Acts of Murder

#2 Random Acts of Deceit

#2.5 Random Acts of Scrooge

#3 Random Acts of Malice

#4 Random Acts of Greed

#5 Random Acts of Fraud

#6 Random Acts of Outrage

#7 Random Acts of Iniquity

Lantern Beach Mysteries

#1 Hidden Currents

#2 Flood Watch

#3 Storm Surge

#4 Dangerous Waters

#5 Perilous Riptide

#6 Deadly Undertow

#3 Safe and Sound

Lantern Beach Blackout: The New Recruits

#1 Rocco

#2 Axel

#3 Beckett

#4 Gabe

Lantern Beach Mayday

#1 Run Aground

#2 Dead Reckoning

#3 Tipping Point

Lantern Beach Blackout: Danger Rising

#1 Brandon

#2 Dylan

#3 Maddox

#4 Titus

Lantern Beach Christmas

Silent Night

Crime á la Mode

#1 Dead Man's Float

#2 Milkshake Up

#3 Bomb Pop Threat

#4 Banana Split Personalities

Saltwater Cowboys

    #1 Saltwater Cowboy

    #2 Breakwater Protector

    #3 Cape Corral Keeper

    #4 Seagrass Secrets

    #5 Driftwood Danger

    #6 Unwavering Security

Beach House Mysteries

    #1 The Cottage on Ghost Lane

    #2 The Inn on Hanging Hill

    #3 The House on Dagger Point

School of Hard Rocks Mysteries

    #1 The Treble with Murder

    #2 Crime Strikes a Chord

    #3 Tone Death

Carolina Moon Series

    #1 Home Before Dark

    #2 Gone By Dark

    #3 Wait Until Dark

    #4 Light the Dark

    #5 Taken By Dark

Suburban Sleuth Mysteries:

    Death of the Couch Potato's Wife

Fog Lake Suspense:

#1 Edge of Peril

#2 Margin of Error

#3 Brink of Danger

#4 Line of Duty

#5 Legacy of Lies

#6 Secrets of Shame

#7 Refuge of Redemption

Cape Thomas Series:

#1 Dubiosity

#2 Disillusioned

#3 Distorted

Standalone Romantic Mystery:

The Good Girl

Suspense:

Imperfect

The Wrecking

Sweet Christmas Novella:

Home to Chestnut Grove

Standalone Romantic-Suspense:

Keeping Guard

The Last Target

Race Against Time

Ricochet

Key Witness

Lifeline

High-Stakes Holiday Reunion

Desperate Measures

Hidden Agenda

Mountain Hideaway

Dark Harbor

Shadow of Suspicion

The Baby Assignment

The Cradle Conspiracy

Trained to Defend

Mountain Survival

Dangerous Mountain Rescue

Nonfiction:

Characters in the Kitchen

Changed: True Stories of Finding God through Christian Music (out of print)

The Novel in Me: The Beginner's Guide to Writing and Publishing a Novel (out of print)

www.ingramcontent.com/pod-product-compliance
Lightning Source LLC
Chambersburg PA
CBHW061423160726

47995CB00003B/735